Cult of Darkness

Novels by Barb Shadow

A Step Into Darkness
Shifting to Black
Invitation to Darkness
Touched by Darkness
Initiate of Darkness
Cult of Darkness

Anthologies

True Ghost Stories and Hauntings, Vol. 1
True Ghost Stories and Hauntings, Vol. 2
True Ghost Stories and Hauntings, Vol. 3

Poetry Collections

Among the Dying Violets
You Were the Music

Cult of Darkness

Barb Shadow

From the Shadows Publishing
Livingston Manor, New York

To My Readers

*Especially the ones who thought
this would be ready in time for a baby shower gift . . .
Oh, you lovely, twisted people!
You're the best.*

Chapter 1

Olivia stepped from the snowy woods into a clearing with a stone firepit at the center. She scanned the surrounding trees. The inverted pentagrams carved into their bark were still visible. She smirked. "Useless boys." Seth and his friend had no idea what they unleashed. What they summoned. But they were no longer an issue. She slid her survival pack onto a large rock at the tree line.

A crow settled onto a branch across from her and a wave of energy pulsed outward surrounding them. She was shielded. Those searching wouldn't find her. Not yet anyway. It wasn't time. There was only one person who would step through that barrier, and he had no intention of saving her.

She wrenched a metal utility shovel from the side pocket of her pack, unfolding and snapping it into place. "Might as well get a fire started." She sighed. "No sense being uncomfortable." She scooped the ashes out of the firepit, piling them to the side. She'd noticed several dead trees that hadn't yet fallen that would burn well. She walked into the woods. Digging her fingernails into the groove of her shovel, she freed its saw blade. She chose a few thinner branches to cut and, on the way back to the firepit, snipped some low twigs off an evergreen. The metal can in her pack held tinder. "Such a boy scout, I am." She snickered to herself as she stacked the twigs and branches and examined her fire starter. "I probably don't really need this with you around, eh, Black? But when in Rome, am I right?"

She glanced over her shoulder at the crow that was watching. One of Black's sentinels. "When will you teach me more, old man?" The blood in her veins chilled, a sensation she'd come to enjoy over the past few days. The demon dripped through her mind.

I have never been a man
And am older than you can imagine

"When will you give me more?"

In due time
We have a loose end to address

Olivia nodded. The loose end was on his way. She blew on the tinder and the sparks caught. The flames roared to life. All she had to do was wait.

Dom stepped over a tree root, his foot sliding in the slush. "Damn it," he muttered, catching himself. His cane was all but useless in the underbrush, and the January thaw didn't help matters. Any footprints or markings in the snow had become wet distortions of themselves, unreadable, and where the trees had shielded the ground, it was nothing but boot-sucking mud. He tossed the cane aside. Shifting his pack, he said, "Slow and steady. Gotta be slow . . . and steady."

A crow cawed in the distance. At least he had his beacon. Or Siren. The demon was aware he was coming and would make sure he found the girl from the news. It didn't matter why. He'd been involved for far too long, surviving when those around him perished. This had to be his destiny. For whatever reason, he'd be the one to defeat the vile piece of shit and send it back to hell. For Amanda. Her brother. And the countless others who'd fallen to this thing over the millennia.

He heard the searchers' voices echo through the woods. They'd gathered in front of the Resnick house, volunteers and officials, little old ladies passing out coffee and donuts before they began. Everyone in bright yellow vests. He'd side-eyed the mass of people as he drove past Wilson and turned up Amsel Avenue, leaving his car behind a 7-Eleven. Far enough to slip ahead unseen, close enough to keep to a probable direction that the girl had taken.

Another crow called.

Olivia's lips curled into a half smile. "Reel him in, brother." She could hear the man in the distance, sense each step he took. Black had toyed with him for a long time, and this was, well, almost the cherry on top. Almost. She thought *why him*, more out of curiosity than caring. Once she had merged with the demon, she understood that the end always justified the means. And she had a thirst for his knowledge. For his *gifts*.

A crunch of branches under foot. A hesitation. The man was closer. Listening. In Olivia's mind's eye, through the crow's eyes, she saw him. Hunched down, waiting. Tense. A crow signaled. Cat, mouse. Hunter, prey.

Are you ready

"I am."

Black eased open a portion of the shield in the direction of the man, a small threshold that would close behind him as he passed through.

The bird issued a final caw.

Dom caught the scent of smoke. Heard the bird. "I'm coming, you bastard," he said. "I just hope you know I'm ready." He shoved branches out of his way and let them spring back behind him. Up ahead, the trees opened to a clearing and, in that space, sat the girl he was tracking.

If the situation were different, he'd be yelling eureka and screaming to the others that he'd found her. Alive. And they'd celebrate.

But not today.

Today, he was silent. Lone. And out to stop a demon.

Olivia used her shovel to adjust the wood in the fire, then jabbed it into the ground. In her peripheral vision she saw the man step from the woods. He was tall, older. Rugged. She kept her eyes focused on the fire as he slid his pack to the ground. In his right hand was a knife.

She waited while he gathered his thoughts, assessed his game plan. Waited while he still believed he was the hunter. "Hello, Devil Slayer." She slowly pivoted to face him. "That is the name of your weapon, isn't it?"

His grip tightened on the handle of his blade.

"Come now, you'll need to be stealthier than that. Or did you mean to make an entrance?"

"I mean to rid the demon that's deceiving you."

She reached into her pocket for a hair tie and twisted her hair into a ponytail. "I know you think that, Dom. Can I call you that? The friend of my friend is my . . . am I right?"

"That thing is no friend to anyone."

Olivia stood and brushed the dirt off her jeans. "Tut, tut. I beg to differ."

"It killed your brother."

"Foster brother. And Seth killed Seth. Unfortunate, but it happens when you mess with things you can't control."

"And you think you're in control?" Dom rolled his eyes. "What about the little boy?"

Olivia squinted at him, a half moment of concentration. "He's alive."

"Is that all you have to say? Have you lost your humanity?"

She shrugged. "It's overrated."

He took a step closer. "Metal darts were shot into his leg. He'll probably limp the rest of his life."

"Like you?" She narrowed her eyes.

"I only want Black. Not you. Don't let him destroy you, too." He took another step, trying to close the gap between them. "Shut the demon out."

"And lose this?" Olivia's eyes went dark and around them the wind whipped up. The fire roared then went out. "You have no idea what it's like."

"I will stop him."

"You can try."

"This ends here!" Dom lunged.

The shield barrier fell.

"It does." Her eyes returned to brown, and her body went slack as Dom landed on top of her. She fell backward, striking her head on the edge of the firepit. She screamed.

"Help! Help me!"

Dom pinned her, his chest against hers.

Voices of the search party could be heard. "That way, men! We've found her! Go. Go!"

Olivia stared directly into Dom's eyes, a smile playing about her lips. "Help! Please help me!" she screamed again. Blood trickled along the side of her head, a red streak through her hair.

He scrambled to hold her arms with one hand while he raised the knife.

"Get him!"

The crowd pulled Dom off Olivia while the sheriff peeled the knife from his hand. He struggled as the men pushed him down, laid across him. Crushed the side of his face into the mud. Random voices came from the crowd, calling him names, talking into radios. "Son of a bitch trying to hurt a young girl." Someone kicked him in the thigh, knotting it into a charley horse. "Murderer."

"It's not what you think," he said through clenched teeth.

"Tell it to the judge," someone said. "You try to convince a jury of that, you lousy piece of crap."

"It was the demon."

A heavyset man with a toothpick in his mouth put his hand on the shoulder of the sheriff. "Trying to get an insanity defense going already."

"That'll never fly," the sheriff responded. "Hope they throw away the ever-loving key."

They held him down and handcuffed him, while Olivia collapsed crying into the arms of one of the volunteers. They wrapped her in a blanket and whisked her away.

The sheriff spoke into his walkie talkie. "We have the girl. Safe. And we've got the perpetrator."

As they made their way out of the woods, a cheer rose from the rest of the searchers and spectators. Olivia climbed into a waiting ambulance with her foster mother as Dom was placed in the back of a police cruiser. People clapped as he was driven away. A little boy with dirty cheeks gave him the finger.

Dark laughter rose through the trees.

Twenty-two Years Later

Chapter 2

The woman entered the Starbucks on County Line Road and went to the end of the line. She dropped the hood of her wool coat and debated what to order. She preferred Dunkin', but proximity was everything. The person ahead of her, a man in a sport coat, stepped to the side and she found herself in front of the display case. She glanced from it to the menu above.

"Frosty morning." It was Mr. Sport Coat.

"Cold as a witch's tit."

The man awkwardly moved on, mid-thought. She'd caught him off guard, and rightly so. She had other things on her mind this morning and didn't need to make idle chit chat with an aging fugitive from Chippendales. Especially at 6:30 a.m.

"Can I help you?" It was the barista. She was slender, in the usual black shirt and green apron.

"Yes, thank you. I'll have the spinach, feta and egg white wrap and a Grande black coffee." She felt foolish. Short, Tall, Grande, Venti. Ridiculous.

"Your name?"

That's right. Here, you weren't an order. They wanted to personalize it. Make sure everyone in the store knew who you were. Or who you wanted to be.

"Ma'am?"

She didn't think she looked like a ma'am, but the kid was most likely from Newcomb Community College, working for pizza and gas money. Everyone over twenty-five looked like a ma'am when you were eighteen. "Rose," she said. "Use Rose."

Sirens began in the distance as they called the next name.

"Jeremy!" Another name or affectation. She preferred to go unnoticed, be the next number in the queue.

Mr. Sport Coat approached the counter. Of course, he was a Jeremy. He could've even been a Chad. She watched as he reached for his coffee and a Rolex peeked from beneath his sleeve. Go get 'em, Jeremy. Try to reel in those fish.

"Fire somewhere," he said to the girl handing him his coffee.

Posh, pretentious and an observer of the obvious. He grabbed a napkin, then stood at their window looking up and down the street. The sirens wailed closer.

"Smoke on the next block. Looks like the New Horizons house is burning."

The baristas craned their necks to see past their station while she waited for her order. She smiled inwardly as the trucks' horns blared, cutting a path as cars pulled to the sides of the street. An ambulance rode in behind them. When plans were set into motion, it was so satisfying.

"Rose!"

She picked up her bag and coffee and took a table by the window, arranging her chair so she could watch the scene. What began as hazy smoke was now black plumes. She could see the flames through the first-floor windows, tall and wild, glowing bright orange against the dark background. Shadows danced as it sputtered and roared.

The firefighters scrambled as four or five men ran from the building. EMTs rushed to get them safely out of the way and began treating them. Oxygen for one, checking another's hand for burns. They'd all gotten out on their own. She assumed they were fine.

But lives were inconsequential. She unwrapped her sandwich and took a bite, closing her eyes. Projecting her mind into the halfway house, she stood in the center of the fire, then moved through the house.

The living room was destroyed. She stepped across the burning boards and could almost feel the searing heat of the flames. Where there used to be curtains, there were strings of fire. Piles of hot ash. Intense heat had bubbled the beige paint off the walls, burned off the wallpaper. The smell was acrid and would have burned her lungs had she actually been standing there. The joys of being a little more than mortal.

She heard a pop and drifted to the kitchen. Glasses were shattering in the metal sink. She could hear the wood boards groaning in the ceiling above and as the beams fell, there was a sudden bright flash. Sparks flew in all directions. It was fully involved. The entire house would be destroyed. If they rebuilt, it'd be at least a year before they'd be open again. And they'd never figure out how it began. Never find the source.

She opened her eyes. Mr. Sport Coat was looking at her. She held up her sandwich. "Delicious."

He took another sip of his coffee, then wiped his mouth with a napkin. "Time to start the day. Bye, ladies."

The baristas waved as he went out the door, letting in a smokey smell on the cold February air.

She wrapped the rest of her sandwich and picked up her coffee, still steaming in its paper cup, and left. One down, and so much more to do, she thought. She dropped the sandwich and the cup in the nearest garbage can. It wasn't delicious and she didn't care for their coffee. She glanced over her shoulder as a thundering snap and crash caught her attention. The second floor of the house collapsed. Firefighters shouted directions over the noise.

She got to the side street and walked five parking spots to her silver car. Hitting the button on her fob, the doors unlocked. She breathed in the crisp air, then sniffed her coat. A faint odor of smoke came from the fibers. "Guess I'll be making a trip to the dry cleaners." For now, though, she had appointments to keep.

Chapter 3

The door to the dorm room flew open and a tall, skinny guy strode in. Paul. "Reverend Anderson! Get your ass out of bed. We've got class in twenty minutes."

"It's not reverend yet, and I prefer pastor." Tom sat up and pulled his blanket across his shoulders, his feet cold on the cement floor. "Don't you ever knock?"

"Don't you lock your door?" Paul dropped his books onto his friend's desk. "And you won't be either if we don't finish out this semester. If you're late again, Peters will have your head like John the Baptist."

Tom rolled his eyes.

"Come on. I want to grab a coffee on the way."

Tom nodded, rubbing the sleep from his face and dragging a hand through his hair. "Gimmie five to grab a shower."

"Three." He pulled an apple from his bag and opened Tom's laptop. "You ever shut this thing down?"

"Do you live here?" Tom walked into the bathroom, checking his face in the mirror. There were bags under his eyes. He shoved the plastic curtain aside, flipped the faucet to hot and waited while the room steamed up.

"We should have been roommates." Bite of apple. "You get any sleep last night? You look like hell."

"Thanks. I guess I was restless."

"Test anxiety. You gotta get that under control, Rev."

Tom stepped under the water and closed the glass door. He soaped up and let the hot water pour over his skin, washing away the nightmares that plagued him. That vague sense of unease when he'd wake and not remember what had chased him through the night. Or what he was hunting. Paul's voice broke through the sound of the water.

"What's with your search history? Damn."

Tom pulled a towel from the plastic loop on the wall and leaned to shut the water off. "What?"

"Your search history is a little twisted, man. Demonology? Rites of exorcism? Binding? Leave that to the Catholics and New Agers. We have a calmer perspective."

"Do we? You haven't heard of deliverance or casting out demons?"

"Please, please. I've heard of snake handling, too, but that doesn't mean I'm going to do it."

He shrugged. "I want to be well rounded. Know what's out there. It's not like they're going to teach it here. Dansville's a little more conservative than that." He didn't say that he'd always felt the need for protection. He wore his cross, prayed to Archangel Michael; he'd even saged the dorm room from time to time, not that he'd admit it. Kind of like Beni in the old Mummy movie. Wear every religious artifact there is and you might be safe. It nagged him his entire life, like something invisible was at his heels. Watching. He pulled on a pair of jeans and started digging through a laundry basket to find a shirt.

"No Black Sabbath. Peters would freak."

"I don't have a Black Sabbath shirt." He pulled on a plain grey tee.

"But I do." Paul lifted his sweatshirt.

"You're nothing but trouble today."

"I'm trouble every day." He took the last bite of apple and tossed the core into the wastepaper basket. "Three points. And what's this Information Network for Victims of Crimes? INVC?"

Tom slung his backpack over his shoulder. "Just a little something I monitor from time to time. Come on, we're going to be late if you get that coffee."

"I need my caffeine."

"And I need to pass."

As they filed out of the room, the laptop beeped. "Hey! You got an email from that INVC place."

"I'll check it later."

Paul picked up his books. "I got us dates for Friday night."

Tom raised an eyebrow.

"There's a party in town." He shrugged. "We're not priests, you know. We can date, get married. Hell, we can even have premarital sex if we repent."

"To hell in a handbasket." Tom pushed him through the doorway. "You sure you're in this for the right reasons?"

"Are you?"

As they jogged down the hallway and out onto the sidewalk, he wondered if he was.

Chapter 4

The silver Lexus pulled into a parking spot in front of the Jameson Realty window. Chris stopped pinning photos of properties onto her rental board to glance at the car. Not the one she was expecting. As the rain created rivulets down the glass, she waited to see who it could be. Montgomery wasn't so large that she didn't recognize most of the cars that drove through town. She smoothed her skirt.

A woman got out, pulling her trench coat tight and hitting the button to open her umbrella to shield herself from the rain.

Chris' eyes widened. She'd know that face anywhere. Even after two decades.

The door to the office dinged as the woman stepped inside.

Olivia closed the umbrella, delicately shaking it in the entryway and propping it against the wall. "Sorry about the drips. Can't control the weather." She turned, recognition apparent on her face. "Christie!" She walked to where her old friend was standing, arm outstretched.

Chris placed the remaining photos on her desk and took the woman's hand. "Olivia."

"Christie Westbrook. Good to see you." She took off her coat, draping it across a chair and depositing her purse on top of it. She looked around the small office. It was cheery enough, for something out of the 1950s. Outdated pale wood paneling on the walls, hunter green carpeting. There was a second desk, although its use seemed to be limited to holding pamphlets and paperwork.

"You, too. I go by Chris now. And it's Jameson."

Olivia raised an eyebrow. "Married the boss?"

"Boss' son."

"Good for you. I never expected to bump into you in Montgomery, even though it's, what, fifteen minutes from our old stomping ground?"

"Yes, about that. Not that we stomped much."

"We did for a while. Had some fun times."

Chris fought a smile. She didn't want to like her old friend; didn't want to give up the grudge she'd carried for so long. "We did. For a while. And where have you been all these years? You up and disappeared after . . . everything happened."

"Seth's death? Yeah. After everything shook out," she pulled a chair away from Chris' desk and sat down, "the trial and all, I needed to get away. I moved in with my grandmother out in Wyoming. Stayed there until I graduated and have been slowly making my way back since." A photo of Chris at a carnival with a tall, blonde man was in a frame on the corner of the desk. Olivia picked it up. "Mr. Jameson, I presume?"

"You know it."

"Very nice."

Chris softened. It felt good talking with an old, old friend, even after what she'd put them through. Or maybe she'd been wrong about what happened. A lot of time had passed, and kids overreact sometimes. Maybe she'd been wrong. "And you? Married?"

She brushed a bit of lint off the leg of her pants. "Only to my work."

"I have to admit, I looked you up once or twice over the years."

Olivia set the frame on the desk and crossed her legs. "I've missed you, too." She paused. "What's Jules doing?"

"She's a lawyer up in Oak Ridge."

"Nice area." She sighed. "I'm glad. We all knew she'd do it."

"The Ouija board predicted it, right?" She shuddered. The board that destroyed their friendship and brought something wrong into her home. Or had it? Could it have been her imagination? A coincidence? At the time she hadn't thought so. She full on believed it.

Olivia laughed. "That toy? Come on, Christie. Our fingers pushed the little thingy around. We all knew it was the only thing she ever wanted."

"You believed it then."

"Please," she said. "I was what, fifteen?"

"What about what happened afterward? The footsteps in my house. The banging."

"You guys never gave me a chance to look into it. Probably the heating pipes in your parents' basement. It wasn't a new building."

Chris took in all that Olivia was saying. It made sense, although she had been terrified as a teen. "What about the scratches on Jules' arm?"

"Haven't you ever gotten a bruise and not known from where?"

"Well, yes, but-"

"But nothing. It could have happened in her sleep, or her cat got her, and the welts didn't come up until later. We were all over hyped and scared ourselves."

"We found the board at her house, but I saw you put it in your backpack to take home."

"It fell out. You know we were in and out of our things half the night." She crossed her legs. "I wish you girls had talked to me instead of freezing me out. It was all explainable." She sighed.

"I was scared. We all were."

Olivia reached across the desk and took Chris' hand. "When were you not? Chris, you thought everything was a demon and out to get you."

Chris reflected. Olivia was right. In her defense, she was brought up that evil hid in every shadow and the only way to keep it out was to be in church every Sunday, every Wednesday, all the holy days and to pray, pray, pray. Go to confession. Say your Hail Mary's. She'd shaken a lot of it off over the years, but still, some nights she'd leave a light on when she went to sleep. She smiled.

"You've got a point. So, you're not into the paranormal anymore?"

"I was for a while. Everyone grows out of their childhood interests at some point. I grew into bigger and better things."

"Is that what brings you into Jameson Realty on this lovely rainy Monday?" Her mood lightened as if the sun had burned off the rain clouds.

"It does. I have my eye on a property. There's a spot that I think will be perfect for what I need."

"You've already decided? Do tell." Chris pivoted to her computer. "The address?"

"I'm not sure of the street number, but it's the old Forest View Apartments site in Freemont."

The only sounds in the office were Chris' fingers on her keyboard and the thunder rolling over the town.

"April thunderstorm. Spring can't be far off," Chris said under her breath. "Here we are." She turned the monitor for Olivia to see the information. "Are you sure? It's been sitting empty for almost twenty-five years. That's not good for any building. You'd have to renovate." She began typing before Olivia could answer. "What do you want to do with it? I may have some other properties that you'd like better."

Olivia reached out and touched the back of Chris' hand. "That's the one I want."

"Are you sure?" Chris' hands hovered over the keys.

"I'm sure. I've done my research, and this is it."

"Of course. We'll do a walk-through before you give your final decision."

"We will, Chris. Absolutely. I'd love to get in there."

"How's Friday, say 11:00 a.m?"

"It's a date."

The bell on the door dinged as a man stepped through. He looked from Chris to Olivia and back. "Excuse me for interrupting.

Mrs. Jameson, something's come up, and I won't be able to make our business lunch today. I'll call later to reschedule." He spun on his heel and was out the door before Chris could answer.

Olivia saw in Chris' mind a hotel room. The *usual* hotel room. And disappointment. "Business lunch?" she smirked. "If I were you, I'd make sure it was in another town."

Chris stammered. Blushed. "No, it's not like that. Roger's a client. Really. The picture of my husband is right here." She picked up the photo, set it down. It slid to fall and she scrambled, grabbing it again. Propping it upright.

Olivia held up her palm. "I'm not here to upset the apple cart. You do you, my dear. And him occasionally." She snickered. "No judgement from me."

Chris opened her mouth, still trying to figure out what to say. And how Olivia knew, but she'd always been intuitive. It was best to change the subject, before she dug herself deeper. "Friday?"

Olivia nodded. "It's a . . . on my calendar." They stood and she gathered her things.

"Looking forward to it."

Olivia tied the belt of her coat and picked up her umbrella. "You know, if you and Mr. Wonderful were interested, I'd give you a discount on," she coughed, "one of the apartments."

Chris didn't know if she should laugh or be offended. "Stop it. He's a client."

"Really. Very discreet." Olivia smirked.

"I'll see you Friday."

Olivia walked out.

Chris waved from the window. Her friend hadn't changed much. And part of her was happy to be meeting with Olivia again on the weekend. She went back to her desk and waited for Roger to call.

Chapter 5

Tom pulled into the Wet Raven parking lot, listening to the gravel under his tires as he made his way to the last available spot. It was grassy and under some low-hanging tree branches. He hoped there wouldn't be slush-mud from the last storm that would slowly suck his wheels into tow truck range.

"So glad you volunteered to be the designated driver tonight. It's been a long week." Paul unhooked his seatbelt.

"I don't remember 'volunteering.' Seems to me I was railroaded."

"You say tomato, I say where's the beer?" He laughed, getting out of the car and stretching. "The girls should already be here."

"And where'd you meet Betty and Veronica again?"

"Carly and Stephanie." He knocked his shoulder into Tom's as they walked along the side of the building. "Over at Newcomb Community College, the student union."

"Good ole NCC. What were you doing at their union?"

Paul cracked a smile. "Looking for dates."

Tom groaned and clapped him on the back. "Leave it to you."

A neon sign sporting a raven blinked to a bucket of water dumping onto an obviously wet and perturbed bird. They were greeted at the door by a bouncer holding out his hand.

"Oh, the woes of a college town," Paul said as he handed over his driver's license.

Tom did the same and they were waved in. "It's your baby face. Maybe next time wear your clerical collar and see what happens." He followed Paul through the crowd, passing the bar and tables. A band was setting up on the far corner stage.

"Hey, girls! Been here long?"

A pretty blonde stood, brushed her long hair over her shoulder and one-arm hugged him, the other hand holding a glass of beer. Paul sat in the chair beside her. The brunette at the table was mid-swallow but waved. There were a pitcher and two extra glasses on the table, all etched with the Wet Raven logo.

"Only a few minutes. Long enough to get started."

"Nice! This is Tom." Paul grabbed a glass and the pitcher. "This is Stephanie," he said, motioning toward the brunette. "And Carly."

"Hey, Tom."

"Tom." Carly raised her glass.

"Ladies." He pulled a chair from the next table and sat down. "Pour me one."

Paul gave a quick nod in his direction, then winked at Carly, his date. "Designated driver."

"I can have one, you ass."

The girls laughed.

Stephanie scooched her chair closer to Tom. "I've never been on a date with a priest before."

"I'm not a priest. I'm going to be a minister."

"Still. It's kind of neat." She ran a finger around the rim of her glass.

The lead singer stepped up to the microphone. "We're Four Dead Monkeys and we're ready to ROCK." The music began and Paul had to slide closer to Stephanie to hear her.

"What?"

"Are you from around here?" she asked.

"Mostly." The pounding of Highway to Hell had him even closer to her, their heads together over their drinks. "I was born in Pennsylvania but moved to Montgomery when I was four. I've lived in Aliton and then Dansville."

"I'm local. Carly, too."

"What?" Carly called over the music. Paul had his arm draped across her shoulders and was drinking his second beer.

Stephanie shook her head.

Carly raised her glass, then leaned against Paul to watch the band.

Stephanie reached for the pitcher across the table and a pendant tipped out of her tee shirt. Tom stared at it as she poured, a memory stirring in him. She blushed.

"My eyes are up here." She smiled again, tucking hair behind her ear. He saw her eyes were as dark as her hair, noticeable even in the dim lighting of the bar.

"No, I," he rubbed a hand across his eyes, embarrassed. "I was looking at your necklace."

Her hand went to the planchette, and she held it out to him. "Are you into the paranormal?" A pause. "No, you can't be. You're religious. Duh. No Ouija boards for you."

He ran his finger over its flat surface. "Religion is kind of paranormal, if you think about it."

Her eyes opened a little wider as it clicked. "You know, you're right. Just on another kind of level." She sipped her beer. "That's pretty deep."

"I think so, too." The crowd clapped and hollered as Four Dead Monkeys started the next song. A rendition of Enter Sandman.

Ouija boards. The memory was out of reach, something old and forgotten, but then it surfaced. Sitting on the floor as a child, the board in front of him. The letters. "I learned the alphabet on a Ouija board."

Her mouth dropped open. "You're shitting me." She touched his arm. "Sorry. Potty mouth sometimes."

"No worries," he said. "You're fine." He shifted in his chair, close enough to Stephanie that he could smell her hair. Berries. "I called it my letter board. I'd sing a little song with it." He closed his eyes as the nursery school tune played through his mind. "It was the alphabet song, but with hello at the beginning and goodbye at the end because-"

"Of the hello and goodbye on the board!" She slapped the table. "That's pretty wild. Kind of spooky, but cute."

Paul leaned forward. "What'd you say about Ouija boards? You summoning demons again?"

The band played louder.

"Just Dr. Peters," Tom said, hiding his laughter with a mouthful of beer.

Paul gave him a thumbs up. He picked up the pitcher of beer and tipped his glass to minimize the foam, then took it with him as he and Carly got up to dance.

"So, your mom let you play with Ouija boards when you were little? That's strange. Mine wouldn't let one in the house."

"My biological mom-"

Stephanie raised an eyebrow.

"Died when I was little. I was in foster homes for a while, then got adopted."

"Gotcha."

"But she was into some weird things. She was a creative type. Artist. I don't know where the board actually came from, but I spent most of my time with it and my imaginary friend."

Intrigued, she placed her hand on his knee. "What was he like?"

Tom searched his mind. It was as if he could almost put his finger on the face, the . . . boy . . . who shared his life, but it was out of reach. At his fingertips, but not. Perhaps because it hadn't been real in the first place. It was his imagination keeping him company while his mother painted. "I don't remember much about him. I did think he'd always be there for me. Always have my back. He was there when my bio-mom died."

"That's so sad." She glanced at the table. "Sad and tragic. I'm

32

so sorry."

"It was a long time ago."

"Still. I hate to hear about when a person's childhood was fucked up. Sorry. Potty mouth." She shrugged with an innocence that melted him.

"You want to get out of here? Take a walk?"

Her hand was on her bag. "Let's go."

"Let me tell Paul."

"Hey, man." He tugged his friend to the side while Carly waited on the dance floor. "Stephanie and I are going to take a walk."

"A walk, eh?" He waved at Stephanie. "You need a condom?"

"What? No."

"You never know. These young college girls, they want to defile us."

Tom laughed. "What are you talking about?"

The bass pounded as colored lights flashed, the band oblivious to anything but themselves and the music they were making.

"You know. Wreck the minister before he gets his collar. A story they can tell their grandchildren."

"I don't think that's something you tell your grandchildren."

"Maybe not. But take it?" He stuck his hand in his pocket to retrieve one and pressed it into Tom's hand. "Celibacy is overrated. And trust me. Defiling is a thing."

"We just met." He shook his head. "Thanks, but I'm not going to need it."

Paul put his hands in the air. "Whatever. I'll see you later," and danced his way to Carly. He gave an up-nod to his friend and mouthed the words "boy scout."

Tom stuffed the condom into his pocket. He and Paul were so different, and that was maybe why'd they been friends so long. He met

Stephanie at the door, put his arm around her waist and ushered her out into the cool April air.

They walked up Remington Avenue about a block, a mist in the air. Stephanie shivered beside him, hands in the pockets of her jacket. "They say it's spring, but I'm not believing it."

There were a few other people outside, mostly hanging around the door to the Wet Raven. "Yeah, it's chilly. Did you want to go back inside?" He motioned back to the bar.

"Nah, not really. It's hard to talk when it gets busy like that."

"That's for sure."

They walked a little farther, crossing Weatherly, slowly leaving behind the bar and convenience stores and making their way toward the more residential end of Remington. Or at least the college apartments and older homes in the area.

"So, tell me about yourself. You know I had an imaginary friend and a Ouija board. What's your story?"

"It's not very exciting," she said. "Born and raised in Newcomb." She looked at the sky. "Graduated from high school and am studying Criminology and Crime Scene Analysis at NCC."

"Get out. How is that boring? What made you want to get into crime?"

She snorted.

"Let me rephrase that."

"Basically, reading the papers, watching the news. I was always into those True Crime novels and documentaries. I wanted to be on the scene, analyze the evidence and have a hand in catching the bad guys. You know, solve the puzzle."

"That's really cool, actually."

"What made you want to be a priest?" She corrected herself. "Minister. My bad."

They'd stopped walking. Stephanie had her back against the brick building of a laundromat. He stood in front of her, shielding her from the wind.

"I don't know. My adoptive family wasn't overly religious. But something always seemed to pull me in that direction. Toward God. To his love and protection. It felt more natural than anything else, I guess. Not as exciting as criminology."

"I think it's cool."

"Do you?"

She wrapped her arms around him, inside his jacket. "Oh, you're nice and warm."

He stepped toe-to-toe with her, his chest against hers and looked into her eyes. "How's that?" He embraced her and she tilted her head so her lips would meet his.

"Well, now," he said, searching her eyes, then kissed her again. First softly, then hungrily, their breath condensing in the cold air. With one hand he brushed the hair away from her face.

She took a deep breath and slowly exhaled. Tom could feel her breasts against him, surging heat through his body. Igniting his desire. He kissed her again, tongue teasing between her lips.

Stephanie ran one hand down his back to his buttocks and squeezed. She whispered, "Forgive me, Father, for I have sinned," and bit her lip.

He laughed. A good, comfortable laugh. An "out with a girl on a chilly night when everything feels crisp and clean" laugh. New. "We should behave. We're on the street."

"We don't have to be."

It took him a second to process what she said. "You want to go back to the bar?"

"Not really." She smiled. "I'd like to chat some more."

As the chill seeped into him, he took her hand. "We can talk in my car."

Chapter 6

Olivia stood beside her car waiting for Christie to pull up. Chris, she reminded herself. Must sound "grown up" after all. Only grown-ups can have affairs with the guy down the street. She adjusted her skinny jeans and shoved her hands into the kangaroo pocket of her black hoodie. She was glad she threw on her duck boots this morning. Winter slush-sludge was everywhere. At least the drive up to Forest View was clean and snow piles were melting along the edges of the lot.

Her phone chimed. The notification on the screen said it was from the INVC. She swiped it away. A little something she'd handle later.

She could tell the area had been well landscaped years ago. The overgrowth from forgotten bushes and hedges now encroached on the building, taking back what had once belonged to nature. The manmade environment never could stand the test of time. It looked as if Jameson Realty had paid someone to cut the grass before the winter but not to do much else. The building itself was faded. Any colors it once had were muted and the brickwork had dulled.

Her attention was drawn to a second-floor window. A shadow. Man-sized. She moved a little closer to the building. The shadow hovered, then retreated into the darkness, merging with other shadows and reflections of clouds on the glass.

A red Nissan Sentra raced up the drive and rolled to a stop beside her. Old. Had to be a 2007 or earlier. Rust was eating the metal at the rear wheel, and she thought she caught the smell of something burnt before the engine quit. Maybe Mr. Jameson wasn't selling as many properties as he should.

Chris let apologies fly through her window before she even opened the car door. "Sorry, sorry. I hate being late, but I had a phone call that needed my attention. Just let me grab the keys. So sorry. Really."

The corners of Olivia's mouth drew upward. Roger, of course. She closed her eyes and saw Chris arranging their tryst for later that day. Rescheduling clients. At least she hadn't tried to change their walkthrough. She would've had something to say, and do, about that. "Oh, I'm sure. Those pressing realty matters." She let her voice trail off as the woman joined her at the front door.

Chris held a ring with a handful of keys attached. "We don't bother with a lock box for some of the sites. The ones that don't get visited often." She jiggled a key in the lock. "As you can see," she said, walking inside, "there's a lot of space. It's a nice set of apartments but needs love and attention."

Dust was everywhere, which she expected, and cracks in the paint and plaster were evident. The air held a musty, stale odor and a water stain marred the ceiling.

"And renovations."

"Well, I told you it's been sitting. There are other, newer, properties that might suit you better. We could wrap up here, visit a couple of others that aren't too far away." Chris was already headed toward the door when Olivia stopped her.

"Why are you trying so hard to not sell this place?" Her arms were outstretched, and she dropped them to her sides. "It's everything I need."

Chris averted her eyes for a moment, gripping her key ring. She took a step closer to Olivia and said quietly, "I don't like this place. It gives me the creeps." Her eyes darted from the hallway to the door to the stairs, to the elevators and back to Olivia.

"I thought you got over that years ago."

"Well, I didn't. The history here," she shivered. "Bad juju."

"Juju."

"Juju." Chris hesitated. "I know I sound silly, Olivia." She twisted the ring in her hands, letting one key after another fall around the circle. Chink, chink. Chink. "But you know it was an asylum originally. For quite a few years. There were deaths on the property. Burials." Chink.

"Oh, well, that can happen anywhere."

"Yes, yes. But then it was left. Abandoned. And Jack Barnes." She exhaled. "I'm sure you've heard about him."

"Wasn't he killed in his home?"

"Yes, but it was after he investigated here. He said something followed him." She stared down the hallway as if waiting for a ghost or ghoul to jump out and chase them. Jump scares. It was always jump scares. Movies, Instagram. She hated it. Set her teeth on edge.

"You don't believe that, do you?"

"What about Joe Paine? The caretaker here? Killed in the office downstairs." She paused for effect. "The old morgue."

"Juju."

"Juju. Or residual energy, as you used to say. Negative stuff. Or bad vibes. I don't like it."

Olivia took a breath. "No worries." She patted her friend's hand. "We won't stay long. I want to get a look at the basement and the upper floors. You can wait outside, if that'd make you feel better." She could handle the juju.

Chris brightened. "Are you sure? I mean, it's my job to point out the important pluses," again, she shuddered, "and any adjustments it might need. Answer any questions you may have."

"I know. I promise not to steal anything or write on the walls with the can of spray paint in my purse." She thought she saw Chris the Gullible hesitate when she said that but then the woman relaxed. Some things never changed. "Go. I'll be fine and if I have any questions, I'll note them for when we're out in the sunshine." She motioned with her hands for Chris to leave.

"Thanks."

Chris went to her car and left Olivia to explore.

Olivia waited in the lobby for Chris to be far enough away. She looked down the first-floor hallway and gathered her bearings. She didn't care about the apartments. To her left was the stairwell and she headed straight for the basement.

She pushed open the fire door.

The energy was stronger here, as she made her way down the hallway to her left. The door to the room she wanted stood open, and she peeked inside. Joe Paine's office. Her office. It was a mess, as she'd expected. She knew the history here. Probably no one wanted to clean it up once the caretaker went a little crazy, a little possessed to be more accurate, and was killed there. The owners put it on the market and washed their hands of it. Of everything. His apartment was farther back, through the office. Easily fixed up and turned into her new living space. But what she needed to see, to feel, was the storeroom at the end of the hall.

Home

She didn't need a blueprint or directions. She could sense where everything was, the layout of the entire property. The graveyard outside, the pentagram etched into the floor upstairs. She could feel it all. The energy called her. Pulsed with Black's essence. His genius. This was where everything began. This was his nexus.

Olivia moved to the storeroom and rested her palm against its door. Wood and chicken wire. That would never do. She'd have to shore up this space. Then, they would work together. Teacher and student, master and apprentice. And she was an apt pupil.

The sound of something clunking on an upper floor caught her attention. It was time to find that shadow.

Olivia emerged from the second-floor staircase and gazed down the hallway. The doors to the apartments were closed and locked. Dull light filtered through a dusty window at its end.

"Come out, come out, wherever you are." Step by step, lingering to listen. "Come here, little mouse. I won't hurt you." She'd send his soul through the portal where Black could feed on his fear. Suck him dry. Tear him to pieces.

And then show her more.

"You don't belong here, little mouse. This is our house."

As she walked, she trailed her fingers along the wall. There were others here, faint remnants of the early residents of the asylum. Hidden well. Deep within the shadows. Cowering. They knew.

She felt a shift in vibration near the elevator and smirked. "I know you're here. You can see me. Why don't we stop this hide-n-seek?" Another step and, there. That was the spot. She inhaled, arms wide. "This is where you died, isn't it, Brian? Where our mutual friend had enough of your foolishness?"

His blood ran cold when the woman said his name. If he had blood. A chill juddered through his being and recognition flooded his mind.

Brian had seen her in the parking lot and, even then, had known the demon was back. He could smell the stench of evil draped across her shoulders like a cape and now, with her not ten feet away, he could see her aura. Dense and dark. He drifted farther into the shadows, through the nearest wall, with all his senses focused on her. This tendril of Black in human form.

He had remained in this space, this realm, since his death. His murder. Waiting. Pacing. Going over and over what he'd done that day that he could have changed. He knew his sister was gone now, too, and it tortured him. If they hadn't investigated this damned apartment building. Or Barnes' house. If they hadn't gotten involved, perhaps they'd both still be alive.

But this was his life. His death. Afterlife. Cold, alone. With the other doomed spirits who walked these halls, but separate. Distant. Waiting. Knowing the demon would return and not knowing how to leave. He wasn't worthy to move on. He'd let everyone down. He should have known the caretaker was in league with this evil. Should have prevented it all. Somehow.

The woman was closer. He'd keep his distance, for now. Continue plotting. Planning. Guilt was a powerful motivator, and he was guiltiest of all.

Two quick toots of a car horn snapped Olivia's attention back to the matter at hand. The walkthrough. She sighed. "If you will excuse me, Brian," her voice dripped with an icy familiarity, "I have other appointments to get to." She pointed her index finger in his direction. "But no worries, dear. I will be back. And we will get to know each other very well."

She jogged down the staircase and out to where Chris was sitting in her Sentra. The sun was high, and she could feel its warmth through her sweatshirt.

"Sorry, sorry," the woman said. "Something's come up. I know you understand. I got a phone call and simply must attend to it."

Olivia smiled her best "not a problem" smile. She knew it was Roger that came up. Or would, once Chris got to his hotel room. "It's fine, Chris. I love the place, and I'll pay asking price. Make the offer, set it up. You've got my number."

"Oh, wonderful. That's great." She fumbled for a pad of paper beside her and made a note. "Thanks for understanding, Olivia."

"Of course. You run along. Don't keep him waiting."

Chris put her car into reverse and frowned, wondering how

Olivia had known.

Chapter 7

Stephanie was waiting on her front steps as Tom pulled into the parking spot in front of her apartment house. It was the typical student rental: older, in need of a paint job, a tromped down dirt path through the flower bed, and yellow and green sorority flags in the bedroom windows. Tom jumped out to open the car door.

"Well, you're quite the gentleman."

"At your service." He bowed. "Where to? Any lunch spot you'd particularly like to hit?"

She gave him a peck on the check before sliding into the passenger seat, then dropped her purse next to her feet and reached for the seatbelt.

"Anything is fine. There's a neat mom and pop sandwich shop in Montgomery that might be fun. I've heard it's good. House of Heroes." She adjusted her seatback. "Whatever you're in the mood for."

"House of Heroes it is." He unclipped his sunglasses from his visor, put them on and shifted into drive. It was a beautiful day. Cold, but crisp. Sunny. No storms in sight.

Tom took the highway, chatting about the weather, finals, and the bands coming to the Wet Raven. It was refreshing talking with Stephanie and made the minutes fly by. Made him brush aside the lingering dark dreams and unease. For today, however, he was out with Stephanie. He put on his blinker and slowed for his exit, then signaled to turn onto Main Street. A man in a bright yellow vest directed him across the intersection to a side street. Main Street was lined with orange cones. Inaccessible.

"Figures they'd pick today to shut things down."

The equipment trucks lined the sides of the street, and one lane was being torn up. "A little early to be paving, right? It's only April. And why would they do it at lunchtime? Looks like we'll have to side-street it to get to the restaurant. Might have to walk a bit," he said, and shrugged an apology. He continued straight until he could take a right onto Pike.

Stephanie pulled her hood strings and snugged it tight. "It's not that cold. And I've got two legs."

"I know." He squeezed her knee.

Pike was a homey street, residential, with a small gas station on the corner. The kind that had one pump, sold beer and smokes and the woman behind the counter said, "Hey, honey," and "You bet, love." Southern hospitality up north.

"I think if you go another two or three streets, we can do a left, right, right thingy and be pretty close to House of Heroes. It's on Davis Ave. I can throw on my GPS, if you'd like."

"Not necessary," he said. "I think we're good." He wasn't sure how close they were, but how hard could it be? A few turns, switchbacks. He didn't need a GPS. Something in him suggested that it might be a good idea, but something louder said no. Perhaps it was a man-thing. Or maybe it was driving with a gorgeous girl and getting to walk with her a little longer than if they'd driven up and parked. Spending a few extra minutes with his arm around her. That worked for him.

He took the left as she'd suggested and found himself on Wilson Lane. Déjà vu slapped him in the face, and he slowed to a stop in front of 235, then made a U-turn in front of the house.

"Whoa." He stared through her window, hands on the steering wheel, taking it all in. The front steps, the screen door. He'd played in that backyard. Watched their neighbor gardening. A pang of sadness caught his heart.

"What?"

Tom came out of his reverie. "Sorry." He sat back against his seat, still eyeing the house beside them. "I lived there when I was little. Before my mother died."

"Oh." Stephanie turned to look at the house, take in what she could from his past. She pictured it more vibrant, without chipped paint and sagging steps. A quaint Victorian with a little boy running across the grass. Letting the screen door slam shut on summer days. Time had left it to decay. "It must've been hard, with you so little. Your mom dying, I mean."

He barely heard her. "Do you mind if I?" He motioned toward the small driveway beside the house.

"No, go ahead."

He parked and got out, with Stephanie following close behind. She took his hand as he absorbed the atmosphere surrounding them.

A hinge squeaked and an older woman leaned out of the front door of the next house. Her hair was in curlers, and she wore a flowered housedress. "You kids interested in 235? My brother's the landlord."

"Excuse me?" Tom asked, stepping toward her.

"Are you kids interested in that house? Just a minute." Her door closed.

Tom and Stephanie exchanged a glance, heard another unoiled squeal, and the woman came down her walk in snow boots and a puffy winter coat. It was black with fake fur framing her face, her housecoat peeking from under its hem.

"That house." She pointed with a bony finger. "You buying it? Looking to rent?"

"No," Tom answered. "We were driving by, and I recognized it. I used to live there when I was a little boy."

"Did you." It was more a statement than a question, the woman pondering the neighbors she'd had over the years.

Tom nodded, squinting at the windows.

"Was that before or after the tragedies?"

It was Stephanie's turn. "Excuse me? There were tragedies?" Her interest in the paranormal piqued. She was fully invested in the conversation. After all, tragedies meant deaths and tragic deaths often pointed to ghosts. She was all ears.

The woman leaned onto her cane. "Yes, ma'am. The woman in that house," un-lean, point, re-lean, "237, she was murdered. The one here," a nod in the direction of 235, "killed herself that same weekend. I always thought they were connected, but I guess the police didn't think so. Heh, what do they know. Always looking for evidence and ignoring the facts." She fished a tissue from her pocket and wiped her nose. "There was a little boy, too, that was left without a mother from it all. So sad." She used the toe of her boot to push a small mound of snow off the sidewalk. Realization drifted across her face like a cloud. "That had to be you. I'm sorry. I am so, so sorry."

Tom gave her a small, sad smile. "Thank you."

Stephanie looked from one to the other, and the old woman said, "I shouldn't have gone on like that. Sometimes I do go on when I shouldn't." Another shake of her head, another shove of the snow.

"It's okay. That was a long time ago." But not long enough. He started piecing things together. The lady next door had been murdered. Murdered. That same weekend? The nice lady. The neighbor. Also dead on Halloween weekend.

"It always gave me the creeps, that house."

"What about it?" Stephanie asked. She shielded her eyes from the sun to scrutinize the exterior.

"Seemed weird to me that the deaths happened right at Halloween. Then, when my brother went to clean out the lady's things," she looked at Tom, "your mother's things, he couldn't. It was like he was *prevented*. Something didn't want him in there."

"So, it hasn't been rented since everything happened?"

The woman squinted at them. "Nope. The bane of my brother's existence. He tried to rent it, sell it. As is, semi-furnished. People look at it and walk away."

"Do you know her name? The woman who was killed?"

A pause in her snow pushing. "It started with an A, I think. Amelia. Amanda. Yes, Amanda, it was. Amanda Harper." She tapped her cane into the cement to punctuate her statement. Pronounce it. She turned and began shuffling back to her porch. Over her shoulder she said, again, "I am sorry."

"Thank you."

Amanda. It was Amanda.

The old woman continued to her porch, muttering. "They really should clean these walks better." She used her cane to knock icicles off her gutter, then waved. "If you change your minds, my brother's the landlord." She went inside.

Tom and Stephanie waited until the woman's door shut before speaking. "Her brother's the landlord," Stephanie said and elbowed Tom.

"Yes." He sighed. "Well. That was something."

"Sure was," she said. "How weird that your neighbor died the same weekend as your mom."

"You're telling me." He gave her hand a tug and they walked between the two houses. "I just want a quick go 'round of the property and then we can grab lunch, okay?"

"Lay on, MacDuff."

As they stepped through a snow drift, Tom said, "Are we quoting Macbeth now?"

"It's something my mom always said. Kind of a 'go on, I'll follow you'?"

Tom's boots crunched through the top layer of ice on a snow pile. "More like 'come at me, bro,' but that works." He steadied himself against the neighbor's house. Amanda Harper's house. Amanda with the snacks Amanda. He could almost picture her face. Almost. A glint of sunlight on an upstairs window in his old house caught his attention. A shadow in the window, then gone. *The* window. The window of the room where his mother hanged herself.

But how did he know that.

For a brief second, he thought he saw his mother, her fingers to the glass. But thoughts can be deceiving. Inaccurate. Wishful.

An icicle dripped, the trickle running down the back of his neck and under his shirt. A chill ran through his skin. Goosebumps. He needed answers.

"Hell is empty, and all the devils are here," he said. Gripping Stephanie's hand, he circled back toward the car.

"More Macbeth?" She waited for him to click the key fob to unlock the doors.

"The Tempest."

"I haven't read that one." She slammed her door shut. "My grandmother would always say something was a 'tempest in a teapot.' Like a bull in a china shop. Same thing?"

He laughed. "No, not really."

"Eh, let's get lunch. I've got a Shakespeare course next semester. Maybe we'll read it then."

They took a couple of side streets and Tom parallel parked in front of a pale blue Victorian. Next Step House. This town had a penchant for Victorian houses. Revitalized, refurbished and historical. The white sign with matching blue letters hung by metal hooks in a black frame. A man sat on the porch smoking a cigarette and nodded to him.

The conversations at his old house still spun through his mind. And *knowing* the window. He had to research it all when he got home. See if he was right. Find the details that escaped him. Find out what happened to Amanda Harper. And his mother.

But, for now he had to find a coin for the parking meter and have some lunch. Tom fished in the console for change. "Hate to ask, but would you have a quarter for the meter?"

"Sure." Stephanie glanced at the man as she dug to the bottom of her purse. "What's Next Step?"

"A halfway house. They help recovering addicts, guys fresh out of prison. Then offer the services they need to reenter society. Gets them on their feet again after hard times."

He scooped up the quarter she offered and smiled. "I owe you one."

They fed the meter and, within half a block, were in front of House of Heroes. A giant sub sandwich was drawn on the window in fluorescent colors. Meaty, with tomatoes and lettuce. It made his mouth water. Tom opened the door and bowed. "Ma'am."

"Thank you, sir." She ducked in ahead of him.

The waitress seated them at a table, leaving menus and a promise to return. Tom watched through the window as some ducks flew by but barely registered the birds. His mind was stuck on the deaths. There had to be a reason, a connection. It was too random. Too coincidental.

". . . wouldn't that be great?"

"Sorry, what?" He unfolded his napkin, letting his silverware roll to the table.

"I was saying it would be cool if we could get into the Harper house to investigate. You know, me, Carly. You." She winked. "It'd be great to have a priest on the team."

The waitress brought a pitcher of water, filled their glasses and said she'd give them a few minutes more.

"I'm," he began, then realized she was kidding. He smiled. "Not sure I'd be good at investigation. Or if that'd be something I'd put on my resume."

Stephanie snorted. "Pastor Tom, ghost hunter. Could be a television series."

It was his turn to laugh.

"But really," she said. She smoothed her napkin, met his eyes. "Why not? It's not like you have to do anything but walk through with us. We'll have a few little handheld voice recorders, a couple of cameras. Nothing fancy. Wouldn't it be great if we caught something? A voice, a clue to what happened? There are more things to heaven and earth, Horatio."

"Than are dreamt of in your philosophy."

"Quite the Shakespearean scholar." She leaned her elbows on the menu and rested her chin in her hands.

"I like the bard. And his quotes."

"Me, too. And the investigation? Will you join us?"

"You don't even know if you can get into the house. Or if someone lives there."

Stephanie shrugged. "Doesn't hurt to ask."

He slid forward on the vinyl seat, his knees touching hers. "Fine. If you can set it up, I'll walk the house with you. See what you do."

"Yay!"

She sat back in her seat as the waitress returned.

"Are you ready to order?" The woman in the red House of Heroes tee shirt and black pants held a pen to her pad.

Tom opened the menu and sheepishly said, "I think we need a minute more."

Chapter 8

The office at Atlas Energy Systems was buzzing. Phones were ringing, printers humming. Mondays were always busy with customers calling in with their problems from over the weekend.

Daniel Mapes got his schedule from dispatch and looked it over. Two calls in Bedford, minor heating issues, maintenance needed, same for Duncan. But his 2:00 p.m. was in Freemont. Forest View Apartments. That had to be a mistake.

He approached the dispatch desk and waited for Mike to get off the phone with a customer. "Hey, man. Can you recheck my 2:00?"

Mike confirmed it. "Forest View."

"Can you give it to another tech?" Daniel rubbed the back of his neck.

"Why? You sick?"

"No. It's," he leaned closer, "you know what it is."

The man looked confused, then his eyes grew wide. He threw down his pen. "Are you kidding me? That was like thirty years ago."

"Twenty-five. But you remember what we felt. Saw. *Heard.*" His hands were shaking. He'd never forget the figure that chased them or the scream that rose up from the basement of the apartment building.

"I know what you thought you saw."

"Cut the shit, Mike. We were there after they closed the asylum, and it was your idea to return to check out the apartments."

"Yeah, but it could've been anything, what we heard. A hurt animal, probably."

"Animals don't scream like that, and you know it." He cringed on the inside; the deranged yell still echoed through his mind late at night. It seeped through his bones. Every nightmare he'd had since they were there included that God forsaken place. "There's only so many chances you get in this life, and I've already used two on that place. Third's the charm, isn't that what they say? If there's anybody else who could pick it up . . ."

"There isn't. The Bedford, Duncan, Freemont areas are yours. I don't have anyone I can spare. It's yours. Just go, do the work and get out. Same as any other job."

"Except it's not."

"You'll be fine. I'm sure of it." He lowered his voice. "Nothing happened there. We heard what we heard, an animal, like I said. And that's what you need to remember. Dan, do you need this job?"

"You know I do."

"Then do it. The contact is a woman." He thumbed through the paperwork on his deck. "Here it is. Olivia Mulvey. If a woman's living there, how bad can it be? You think she's shitting the bed every night, some boogey man at her bedside? Whatever the stories were, whatever you believed, it's gone now."

"Maybe." He guessed it could be, but it didn't make him feel any better.

"Good. You can tell me about it tonight over a couple of beers. Add to that belly of yours."

"Yeah, man. As if you're going to hit the cover of GQ anytime soon yourself. Sure." He gathered his assignments and went to load the van.

Olivia was in the lobby when she saw the Atlas van pull in. On its side was the famed Titan, but holding a boiler on his shoulders, with some other HVAC parts, instead of the celestial sphere. "Chee-sy." She went back to looking through the last two boxes the movers had dropped off while she waited for the guy in the maroon Atlas shirt and khakis to grab his things and come in.

He cleared his throat. "Miss Mulvey?"

"That's me." She stepped around the box on the floor.

Another cough. "Dan, from Atlas. You called with a problem?" He glanced toward the stairwell, back at her.

"Olivia," she said. "Name's Olivia. Yes, I called. I'm having an issue with the heat in one of the rooms. Everywhere else is fine, but my apartment is pretty chilly. You can imagine how that's a pain with it still being cold outside."

"Yes, ma'am." He shifted his weight from one foot to the other. "I can definitely troubleshoot that for you. It's most likely either a blockage in the ductwork or a malfunction in that room's thermostat. I'm sure I can have you up and running well in short order." First foot, the other.

"That's great."

"And which of the apartments is it?" He looked past her down the hallway.

"Mine. The one in the basement."

He tensed. The basement. Exactly where they'd been when they heard the screaming howl that sent them scrambling for their lives. Right on those stairs.

"I can show you, but would you do me a favor?"

He tried to clear his throat once more, but he'd gone dry as desert sand. "Sorry, what?"

"I was wondering if you would carry one of these boxes downstairs. The movers," she dropped her hands to her sides, "you know movers, they never get things exactly right. They left these up here and I need them downstairs."

Dan shot another look at the stairwell. "Um, yes. Sure." He picked up the larger box.

Olivia took the lighter one and indicated toward the stairs. "It's this way."

"Would you mind if we used the elevator?" His heart was beating harder. Maybe from exertion, he told himself. He was definitely out of shape. Let it be from lifting something heavy. So far things were normal. The woman was friendly enough and she didn't seem to be hunted by anything dark. He could be overreacting. PTSD-ing. God knew he'd battled a ton of anxiety over the years.

"I've never done that, but we can. Good to know if it's working, I'd say."

Olivia touched the down button and the elevator doors opened. The motor whirred to life, and they rode to the basement without incident, both staring at the panel until it lit up with a B. Olivia exited, maneuvering her box sideways through the small doors. "Follow me."

Dan followed. His mind flashed to when he and Mike had broken in and wandered through the apartments after the caretaker had been killed. They'd walked this hallway. He'd touched these walls. And upstairs. Damn it, they'd been upstairs where the pentagram was on the floor. Used the Ouija board. The heaviness of the air brought it all to the forefront of his mind.

He forced away the thought as best he could. It was different now. Miss Mulvey didn't seem afraid. Olivia. She was happy to be living down here. Mike was right. He needed to get out of his own head and see reality.

"You can drop the box anywhere," she said as they entered her office. "And the heating issue is back this way."

Dan did as she said and walked into her living room.

He cut the power to the system, checked the air vent in the living room and inspected the one in the bedroom while Olivia went upstairs to do whatever it was she did there. Owned it, caretaker, he wasn't sure. His hands trembled as he held the screwdriver.

Enough, he thought. Enough of that. He hung his hands at his sides, shaking them. He was there to do a job. Nothing had jumped out at him and obviously *she* was fine. He'd finish, like Mike said, leave, and they'd meet for beers later to laugh about it. He just wished there was a window. Something to let in the light of day, let him see a bird or two fly by. Something to distract him from the fact that this building had been an asylum. That her office had been the morgue.

He shuddered. But, with an old building, that'd happen. You'd have rooms that were used for other things, where people had died, even. He'd heard of people who bought funeral homes and moved into them.

Another shiver. Yeah, but they made a movie out of that scenario. Didn't end well for the folks involved, either.

He pulled the cover off the vent. The thing was caked with dirt and lint. That was probably a good part of the heating problem. Can't get heat if it can't blow through. He set it on the floor beside his bag and picked up his flashlight. A quick look inside the duct to make sure there was no obvious blockage and he'd be in business. Get in, get out, on to the next.

He shined the light into the duct and farther back, it'd be a reach, was something. Sticks and who knew what. An old animal nest perhaps. Clicking off the flashlight, he dropped it into his bag and put on a glove. He stuck his arm into the duct, pressed his body against the wall and reached into the pile. He got his fingers behind the mound and shuffled it forward, to the mouth of the vent.

It was bones. Small animal bones.

He swallowed, refusing to give in to the creepy vibe this place held for him. It wasn't like he hadn't found bones before. Animals sometimes had a cache, food for later. Leftovers from kills. Not that they'd be killing other animals within ductwork. Even though this seemed like a lot. Multiple kills. Various species.

Striding into Olivia's bathroom, he found her trash can and, luckily, it had a bag. With a sweeping motion of his hand, he dropped the bones from the vent into the can, then tied the bag shut. He finished his inspection, then cleaned the cover with a wire brush. He flipped the switch and waited for the system to call for heat.

Warm air poured from the vent. Hurrah.

"You fixed it!"

Dan jumped. He hadn't heard her walk into the room, let alone be right behind him. "Whoa," he said, his hand on his chest. Heart pounding. "Gotta say, you startled me." He straightened.

"My bad."

"It's all good. I was focused on the heat." Putting the last screws into the cover, he mentally kicked himself for being so ridiculous. "It looks like you're good to go. Quick and easy. Oh, and there was a pile of bones in the vent. I dumped them into your trash."

"Bones."

"Bones. Rodent, bat, I don't know what. Quite a cache. Between that and a gummed-up cover, it choked off your heat."

"Glad we're good now."

"Let me get everything together, throw my tool bag into the truck and I'll write up your invoice. I'll be right back."

"Sounds good."

His bag hit the floor of the van with a thud. He took his aluminum clipboard off the dashboard and fished a pen out of his cupholder. The sun shone through his windshield, warming him and making him feel better about the day. It'd gone well. Easy, in fact. The biggest speed bump was his own overactive brain.

He wrote the invoice. Service call and diagnostic, labor. $157.40.

The lobby held a different feeling for him as he walked inside. He took a moment to look around, breathe in. Even when he turned to the stairs, his unease had lessened. Not disappeared but definitely eased. Yeah, he needed to get over himself. His biggest stumbling block. All those years of being afraid of his shadow after running out of this place and he was taking charge now.

It felt good.

He took the stairs, clipboard in hand. Almost wanting to move a little faster but keeping his rationality and walking into her office.

Olivia was on the phone and motioned for him to sit down.

"Yes, yes. Good. Send me the paperwork. I'll talk with you later." She clicked to end the call and put her phone on the desk. "How'd we do?"

Dan held out the bill. "$157.40."

"Not bad at all." She took out her checkbook.

"I've got to admit. Being here shook me a little."

"Oh?" She looked over her glasses at him, then went back to writing. "Why is that?"

"When I was a kid my buddies and I were here. Checking the place out after the asylum closed and again later on. After the caretaker and that other guy died. Scared the heck out of us."

"What happened?" She sensed it in his mind. The residual fear. The panic. It was time for some confessions. Speak up, Dan.

"Oh, you know. Kid stuff. Trying to scare each other. We found a bunch of stuff on the second floor. Black candles, a pentagram. A Ouija board." Even telling her brought back the sense of unease. "Tried it, too." He swallowed. Didn't know why he was telling her.

"Really. Was it anything like this?" She reached under her desk and brought out a wooden Ouija board. "It's been here a long time."

The pine board could have been new, or a hundred years old. He couldn't tell. The varnish reflected the light of her desk lamp, the stenciled letters as black as ever. Freshly painted, old as the hills.

He sat up straight. "If you don't mind me saying, you may not want to keep that around. Those things can be dangerous."

"Only in the wrong hands." She signed the check and handed

it to him.

The temperature in the room fell as Dan tucked the check into his clipboard.

"You say you used the Ouija board you found when you were here?"

He stood. "We did."

"Then you probably met a friend of mine."

Dan turned to see a shadow standing behind his chair. The shadow from his nightmares, seven feet tall and dark. So very dark. His knees buckled and he caught himself on the edge of her desk. Its red eyes connected with his and it grinned. *Grinned.*

He ran. Past the thing, up the stairs, through the lobby and out into the parking lot. Grappled with the door handle to the Atlas van and climbed into the driver's seat. He threw the clipboard to the side, fighting with the keys to get into the ignition. He dropped them once, fumbled then started the engine. Throwing it into reverse, he hit the gas, turning the wheel. He shifted into drive and plowed forward. As he hit the first curve, he looked into his rearview mirror for one last glance at Forest View.

The demon glared at him from the back seat.

Dan felt the gas pedal hit the floor under his foot and the van sped as he tried to get control. Tried to turn a wheel that wouldn't turn. He jammed both feet onto the brake pedal with all his might but the van accelerated.

The Atlas van crossed the main road at fifty miles per hour and slammed into a utility pole. The horn sounded for a full minute after impact, as the sirens in the background took over.

Black stared into Dan's eyes as the life left his body, relishing in his fear. And then the demon reaped his soul.

Chapter 9

The afternoon sun shone into Tom's dorm room, threatening to blind and broil him at the same time. He cranked the handle, opening the vertical window in the middle, then lowered his blinds. He understood that the dormitories kept their heat going through the end of the month, but on sunny spring days, whoa. Now able to focus on and see his computer screen, he googled Amanda Harper and the Montgomery address. Anything would work. Old newspaper records, local papers. Whatever he could find.

Thank God for the internet, he thought. A list of articles was on his screen in a fraction of a second.

Local Ghost Hunter Found Dead – Montgomery Sentinel

Amanda had been a ghosthunter?

A team member of Out of the Dark Paranormal was found dead in her home in Montgomery yesterday. Police are investigating the possibility of foul play.

He clicked on the next article. It was a snippet from the Aliton Gazette.

Local Woman Dead in her Home
Victim of foul play or the ghosts she sought?

And the next.

Deaths at Forest View Apartments – The Freemont Tribune

Members of Out of the Dark Paranormal had been investigating at Forest View Apartments when the caretaker, Joseph Paine, allegedly killed Brian Harper and severely wounded Dominic Russell. Amanda Harper, the victim's sister, appears to have shot Paine in self-defense. He also died at the scene.

Tom tipped backward in his chair, using his knee under the edge of his desk to keep himself upright. He ran his hand through his hair. The name was like a flashing neon sign, and his thoughts ran wild. Dominic Russell. There couldn't be two of them, could there? Maybe he read it wrong.

He checked the article once more, then minimized the window and pulled up his email from the INVC. The one that informed him Russell would be released from prison next month. Russell, the man who tried to murder his foster sister twenty plus years ago. The words on the screen swam in front of his eyes. His mind spiraled.

Tom typed "Dominic Russell" into the search bar. Articles from the attack on Olivia sprang up, the trial. The usual vague mentions in local newspapers. Until he saw one posted by the Willow Tree Weekly. It likened Russell's claims of innocence to Parker Davies' "Dark Entity Defense."

What the hell can of worms had he opened? Who was Parker Davies?

He dove in further. A man named Jack Barnes was brutally murdered and his best friend, Davies, was put on trial. The man had maintained his innocence throughout and blamed it all on a demon that Barnes had gotten involved with at the abandoned New Castle Asylum in Freemont. While ghost hunting.

Out of the Dark Paranormal, which Amanda and her brother Brian belonged to along with Russell, had investigated the Barnes house. Then, Forest View Apartments.

Tom planted his feet squarely on the floor. It read like a horror novel, and he was the detective, putting every detail together from multiple sources. But this was crazy. He didn't know what to believe. Could Russell be a serial killer? After all, he'd been at the scene of a number of murders. And he tried to kill Olivia.

Or was he on the level and innocent? Not truly innocent, though. He'd been ready and willing to kill a fifteen-year-old girl. But why?

Nothing tied to his mother that he could find, other than living next door to Amanda. Maybe that was a big coincidence.

But he didn't believe in coincidence, only divine synchronicity. Everything happened for a reason, but damned if he knew what the reason was.

His door flew open and Tom jumped, knocking his chair over. "Damn it."

"A little tense?" Paul asked.

"A little. A knock would be nice."

"I did. You didn't hear it." Paul picked up the chair, rolling it to the desk. "Deep in your paper or what?"

"Oh, hell. I haven't started it." He dropped his pen onto the pad of paper where he'd been taking notes, then shoved the pile into his desk drawer.

"Not good, Rev. You've only got till 11:59 tonight to get it submitted."

Tom nodded.

"It's thirty percent of your final grade."

"I know, I know." Tom shuffled papers and books on his desk. "I'll make it."

"If I can help, let me know. Otherwise, I'll be over here." He flopped onto Tom's bed and began flipping through his phone.

Chapter 10

Dom dumped his plastic tray and added it to the stack of empties. The chicken was dry and the potatoes crumbly. Watery green beans leaked out of their compartment. If he were sentenced to a thousand years, he'd never get used to the food.

The loudspeaker crackled and a voice announced, "Count." As usual. As always. He proceeded to his cell, 227 B, and waited on his bunk. The officers eventually came through checking heads, making sure everyone was there. He wouldn't miss 'Ole Aarondale. A few more weeks and he would be on the outside once again. Back at life. Back at . . . The buzzer signaled that all was well. No one had escaped and it was time for evening activities. Today was Wednesday and he had some television time coming. He rose, stretched and headed to the common room.

His buddy Frank was playing solitaire while the 6:00 p.m. evening news played in the background. The same faces milled around. Same shit different day, as they would say. He picked up the remote. Fingering the well-worn buttons, he asked, "Anybody care if I change the channel?"

A few "Nahs," and "Mms," came in response. Nothing definitive. Non-committal. He pointed the remote at the television as a breaking news story hit the screen.

This is Sam Ellis with WBBL-TV reporting. A fast-moving blaze engulfed the Next Step House in Montgomery this morning, sending residents scrambling to safety. Eyewitness reports stated they had never seen a fire progress through a building so quickly. Emergency services evacuated several buildings surrounding the home. Miraculously, none have been touched by the flames. Fire Chief Warren Mason stated that they will be investigating the source of the inferno and that the possibility of arson has not been ruled out. This is the second halfway house fire in as many months, the first being the New Horizons building in Newcomb. Stay tuned to WBBL-TV for the latest developments in this breaking story.

In other news, in Freemont, an Atlas technician was found dead in his repair truck, victim of an apparent heart attack. The man . . .

Dom muted the television. "Another fire." He stared at the quiet screen, not really seeing it. Some group saving puppies from a puppy mill went by and a guy winning a hot dog eating contest. "Huh." He wasn't concerned. Wasn't upset. He knew what was waiting for him and was well aware of the warning it was sending.

"That's where you were set to go, wasn't it?" Frank said without taking his eyes off his cards. Red queen on black king. Next group. Two of clubs on three of hearts.

"Sure was."

"And that first one. You were scheduled there, too." No match. A flip of the pile.

"Yup." Dom sighed.

"That sucks."

"Sure as hell does."

"Someone doesn't want you out." Frank laughed, a dry-throated wheeze. "Got enemies on the outside?"

"You might say that." Dom left the room. It was time to concentrate a little harder, focus with more intensity. His plans were coming together, and, by his release date, he'd be more than ready.

"Stay away from those dark arts. They'll get you every time." Frank called after him, his laughter escalating into a coughing fit.

"Not this time," Dom muttered as he returned to his cell to think.

Chapter 11

She waited in the dark empty room, eyes closed. Sensing. Feeling. Watching. He'd be coming soon. He was striding down Weatherly, almost to the intersection with Pages Lane, then three buildings down and he'd cross the street in front of her. There was plenty of time.

Olivia concentrated, zeroing in on the man's movements. His agitation. What he was looking for. What he needed. And how she'd bring him in. Like an anglerfish, she'd lure him. And, with Black's help, she'd have him.

She focused on the man's mind. He'd lost his job and was itching for a fight. For something. Like an addict late for his next hit, he was in need. He turned the corner and Olivia switched on the shop lights. A green neon sign glowed in the window. Top Hat Tattoo.

She saw him through the window. Burly. Bald. He opened the glass door, and a bell chimed. Olivia stood beside the table of tattoo flash books, her black leather pants and fishnet top accentuating her figure. Her hair, dark and fringed around her face, pulled into a high ponytail, clinched it.

"First client of the night. Come on in." Her ankle boots clicked on the tile floor as she stepped forward.

Reilly let the door swing shut behind him.

"What are you looking for? Skull and dagger? Perhaps 'mother' in a heart on your ass?" She pointed him to a chair. "Is this your first time? A little virgin skin?"

He cracked a smile. "Virgin nothing." Taking off his denim jacket, he slid up the sleeve of his shirt. His ink was apparent. Skull and roses, barbed wire around his upper arm, a tribal band.

"Tsk, tsk. Those are some crappy tats. Get 'em in prison?" She pulled over a rolling stool and sat next to the chair.

"Yeah."

"Were you in long?"

"Long enough. Been out a few months. Someone must've whispered in the governor's ear."

A sly smile played about her lips. "Someone must have."

He walked around. Posters of people getting inked hung on the walls amid photographs of the work done at the place. "I don't remember this shop being here. You been open long?"

"My first night." She bent forward to adjust her shoe and he took a long look down her shirt.

"You alone here?"

"You need more than one person to shove needles in your skin?"

"Maybe. You sure you got the skills?"

"Oh, I can assure you I'm skilled at what I do," she said in a sultry voice. "Are you going to tell me what you want so we can get down to business?"

Reilly walked up to her, gripping her arm, his face so close to her ear she could feel his stubble. His breath was hot on her neck. "I'm ready. Are you?"

Olivia turned, a darkness forming in her eyes like thunder clouds, the energy in the air electrified. One by one, his fingers were peeled away from her wrist. He watched, jaw slack.

"That's right, Brutus. I think you need to know who's in charge here."

A tall shadow formed beside her, and a force shoved him backward. He fell into the black leather recliner.

"Now, I want you to listen. No more games."

"Wha, what was," he stammered.

She tilted her head to the side. "You need a job. I need

someone to be eyes and ears when I'm busy. A distraction with muscles. You're a thug and that works for me. I pay well. Really well. But get out of line and the punishment's worse than getting your ass strung up a flagpole. Worst nightmare shit. Got it?"

"You want a bodyguard."

She laughed out loud. "I don't need a bodyguard, dear."

"You running drugs or something? This shop a front for something else?"

Olivia smirked. "This," she spun, waving an arm toward the walls, "is an illusion. A mind fuck. A little fun to draw you in, Brutus."

"My name's Reilly."

"Reilly." She shrugged. "What's in a name?"

"What are you, really? Something pushed me, but nothing was there."

"I'm a little necromancer with great expectations. A wee girl with a bit of power. Quite a bit, actually."

"I don't know."

"It's now or never. I don't make an offer twice. Waiver and the opportunity goes to someone else." And you'll be dead, she thought. That's how these deals worked. Sell your soul now, dearie.

He hesitated. Bodyguarding some bitch was one thing. Drugs were another. But whatever this was, he didn't get it. He swore something pushed him and what the hell peeled his hand away. She must've slipped him something. A contact mickey. That must be it. Like those twenty-dollar bills people find laced with fentanyl. His eyes searched the shop to find what she had used. That had to be why his heart was beating so hard, underarms sweating, even though the room was cold.

"If you'd like to see more of what I can do, that's fine, too."

"Maybe I would." He'd call her bluff. Make her perform and screw up.

She thought for a moment. "Here," she said. "A little taste of what you're getting into." She took his head in her hands and pressed her lips to his. Her mouth held an intoxicating darkness, and the longer she kissed him, the more it felt as if thousands of needles were puncturing his skin. Piercing his mind. The sheer power of it all was like a magnet to his desire. Pain and pleasure contorted him, while Black's energy flowed through his veins.

She tore away, leaving him panting, hanging onto the edge of the chair. White knuckled. Pale. His fingers left half moons dug into the faux leather.

"My boss is from another plane. You work for me."

"I-"

"There is no other choice."

He hesitated, the taste of power lingering on his tongue along with something disturbing. Titillating and terrifying. Like having his cock rock hard but knowing she'd rot it off or chop it in two. Knowing and yet unable to pull away. "You taste unholy."

"Unholy is such a strong word." She walked around the shop, giving him time to come down. Relax. Think about her offer.

He stayed in the chair, still gripping the armrests. He felt as if he'd been tied down, and taken to the edge, just to be left hanging. He wanted more but was afraid to move. She was a fucking black widow.

The feeling dissipated and Reilly ached for it to return. Like chasing a cocaine high. "I'm in."

Olivia stood. "Meet me at Harmony Hills Cemetery on Thursday. 3:30 p.m. You can move into my apartment house in Freemont on May first. Now go. I have work to do." She walked to the counter, done with whatever business transaction this had been.

"That's like three towns over. My parole officer-"

She waved him off. "I'll handle your P.O." Without looking up, she added, "Show up and you'll have more than you've ever dreamed. Stand me up and you'll burn."

He didn't doubt that in the least. He got up, weak-kneed, and shuffled to the door. "Do I at least get a tattoo?"

"You're already marked."

\#   \#   \#

Reilly crossed the street and stopped under a streetlight. He looked back toward the shop. The lights were out, and any remnants of Top Hat Tattoo were gone. *Gone.* Maybe somebody slipped him something at the bar. He rubbed the back of his neck, then noticed a small mark on the inside of his wrist. The tattoo of a crow.

Chapter 12

Paul zipped his jacket as he and Tom jogged down the sidewalk between Joshua and Steinman Halls, skirting other students on their way to their respective classrooms or dorms. "You know it was damned nice of Peters to give you a break and let you turn in that paper late."

"Damned nice." Tom clutched the folder that held his paper, fifteen pages of fluff instead of content, that he hoped would float him till the final. He'd buckle down and study hard for that. And the others. Then, graduation.

"You're mocking me. Why do I get the feeling that you're mocking me?"

"You're mocking meeee," Tom said in as close to a high-pitched whiny girl's voice as he could get.

"Asshole."

Tom punched Paul's arm as they turned the corner and went up the steps of Hart and through the glass doors. Taking the stairway to the right, they went down a floor, where the hallways were carpeted in red and the lighting was muted. Various doors had brass name plates. Peters was the last in the dead-end.

"It's so quiet in here. I half expect the librarian from Ghostbusters to come out of the wall and shush us."

"That's probably Peters' secretary," Tom said.

Paul's snicker was trying to expand to out and out laughter, but he rested his forehead against the wall while Tom walked the final five feet to the door with his professor's name.

"You'd think he would've let me submit online."

"It's a tactic. He gives in to let you hand it in late, with demerits, and you have the embarrassment of placing it gingerly in his hand. Don't do it again, slap on the wrist," Paul said.

Tom knocked on the door before slowly opening it and sticking in his head. Luckily, only the secretary was in and, equally lucky, she didn't look like a librarian. He held up the folder with his paper. "I'm dropping this off for Dr. Peters?"

The woman pointed at a box on the side counter, filled with folders similar to his. He dropped his on top, then reconsidered and tucked it in the middle of the stack. No need for it to be graded too soon.

"Thank you," he said as he backed out of the door, bowing. "Thank you. Thank you."

Paul was reading the postings on the bulletin board. "Not sure why they pin anything up in this light. Makes it hard to read."

"Nothing up there worth reading anyway," Tom said. "Dinners, recognitions. Conferences. Boring."

Paul tucked his hands in his pockets as they went back up the stairway to sunlight. "You're going to be part of that boring life someday soon, you know."

"Nah."

Paul looked at him, an eyebrow raised as high as it could go, and he took the rotating door, chasing Tom around twice for good measure.

When he exited, Tom said, "Putting the rev in reverend."

They rounded the corner into the quad. Dr. Peters was speaking with another professor beside a stone wall. Tom pulled the edge of his hood across his cheek and ducked his head as they walked past.

"Thomas."

Dr. Peters' voice. He was nailed. Tom took off his hood and turned. "Dr. Peters."

"I assume you're coming from my office."

"Yes, sir. My paper is in the stack."

The man nodded and returned to his conversation. Tom almost fell against Paul as they broke into a run to the parking lot. Tom clicked his fob to unlock his car doors, and Paul bent in to move old fast-food bags and water bottles to the back seat.

"Geez, Rev. Slob much?"

"It happens."

"Survival on fast food is not survival, my man."

"And you're such a gourmet? Aren't you the king of the burger? AKA the Burger King?"

Paul stood, hands on the roof of the car. "That's Emperor Burger to you." He threw a wadded-up bag at Tom. It bounced off the next car and rolled. "Off with you, servant. Attend to the garbage."

Tom scooped up the bag, ready to throw it at his friend, when he noticed a little girl and her mother talking a couple of cars over. Probably a TA. Maybe a secretary. They were staring at the bushes near the walkway.

"Mommy, he's so pretty. I want him."

The little girl shoved her blonde curls off her forehead. She couldn't have been maybe four or five years old. Tom saw a small, black cat under the branches.

"I'm sure he belongs to someone, honey."

"He's got no collar."

"He's a stray and probably full of parasites and diseases. Besides, black cats are bad luck. Come on. We've got to go. Maybe he'll be here the next time you come."

The girl pouted a small pout. "Doubt it." She climbed into the blue sedan. Her mother secured her seatbelt, and they drove off.

"You getting in or what, dude?" Paul asked from inside Tom's car. "I'm so hungry I'm about to start going through these bags."

"Go ahead." Tom's attention was focused on the kitten. It was sleek and black and staring at him. He moved a few feet closer, bending onto one knee. There was a hint of an image, an impression, that nagged at him. That word on the tip of your tongue, that face you should remember. He inched forward. "Hey, kitty."

The memory stabbed him. He had a cat when he was little. Played with a cat. But it wasn't just a cat. It was Jetty. Jetty the cat; Jetty the boy. Jetty the shadow. Tom broke out into a sweat, his stomach bunching into a knot. Jetty, his best friend. Jetty who knew things and caused things to *happen*.

Bad things.

The memories didn't flood the basement of his mind; they became a tsunami wrecking everything in its path.

The bad things he hadn't seen as a child. Hadn't understood. What happened to his mother. Amanda. Seth. Flashbacks. Seeing through his eyes, through something else's. Taking the shadow's hand as his mother backed away calling his name his name. *Come on, Tom Tom. Come with Mommy.* Stabbing the shard of glass into Amanda. Had *he* killed her? It couldn't be. He was five. It was the other thing that had existed in his mind.

He squeezed his eyes shut but still saw her lying at the bottom of the stairs. The memories had always been there, in the back of his mind, held tight in a vise. Hidden from him by . . . what? Jetty? His own psyche? The hold was loosening.

And his mother. Taken from him, along with his emotions for her. His love. That came back in a torrent, too, rushing in and creating a cavern of loneliness within his chest. He was sinking. Drowning, but twenty years later.

Mom, why didn't you save us? Why? It hit hard and fast and fresh.

His stomach heaved, but he held the vomit down.

The best buddy who was supposed to be with him forever, who promised to protect him. The thing he called *Daddy* . . . stole everything.

And left him.

For Olivia. So hungry for anything paranormal. So open.

Oh, God. His imaginary friend had been real. A master manipulator. A commander of lies and destruction. And the evil latched onto his foster sister. The demon called *Black*.

He stood, legs weak. The kitten ran off to chase birds near the dorms, oblivious to his pain.

All he was left with were questions and he needed answers. He had to find Olivia.

"Rev, you okay?"

Tom sat, hands on the steering wheel. White knuckled. Pale, in a cold sweat.

"No, man. I'm not." He faced his friend. "Watching that cat, I don't know. Triggered some deep ass PTSD." He was shaking now, the steering wheel a lifebuoy anchoring him. "Things I didn't know. Did know. Didn't remember, oh, my God." His tears streamed and he pressed his forehead against the wheel. "I was five, man. Only five." His voice trailed off, taken over by heavy sobbing.

Paul watched his friend, not knowing what could have happened when he was a child. He put an arm around Tom and pulled him to his chest. Paul held him, the gear shift sticking into his ribs.

After a few minutes, Tom eased up and wiped his face. "Your shirt's wet." He looked out the windows to see how big a crowd he drew.

"Your fly's open."

Tom checked. It wasn't. "Asshole."

"Always." He sighed. "You want to talk about it?"

"Not yet."

"Had to ask."

"Yeah." Tom exhaled, still trying to make sense and order of what he remembered. A swirl of people, places and emotions running through his mind.

"So, are we going for lunch?"

"What?"

"We were heading for lunch. You know, Rev, that meal in the middle of the day. The one we all adore and look forward to?"

"You adore every meal."

"My point exactly!" He examined his watch. "We still have forty-five till class. Come on, we can make it without a problem. I'm starving."

Tom shook his head, grateful for his friend and his appetite. He reached into his pocket for his keys, and they headed off to find lunch for Emperor Burger.

"I think what your problem is," Paul said between bites, his Whopper dripping sauce into its paper wrapper, "you need to get laid." He set the burger down on the table, pulling every napkin out of their bag. He wiped his mouth.

"What?" Tom sipped his coffee, wincing as it burned his lip.

Paul's hands were in the air, mimicking scales. "Wildly insane PTSD," he lowered his left hand. "Blue balls." His right hand dropped like a rock, hitting the table, while his left went into the air above his head. "Get laid." He smiled.

"I don't need to get laid."

"Rev, we all need it. Don't deny your primal urges."

"Didn't your mother tell you not to talk with your mouth full?"

"Always," he said. "I've got condoms if you need." A swipe of his mouth with a napkin, a wipe of the table where his ketchup had dripped.

"I still have the bar condom."

Paul's eyes widened. "No, Rev. Never use a bar condom. Bad juju."

Tom snorted, almost choking on his coffee. "Asshole. The one

YOU gave me."

"You still have that?"

Tom nodded. He picked up a plastic straw and stirred his drink.

"Oh, man. That confirms it."

"What?"

"Blue balls."

Tom wadded up the burger wrapper and threw it at him. "Come on. We're going to be late." As much as he needed to listen to the day's lecture and review for the upcoming test, he knew he wasn't going to hear a word.

He had to find Olivia.

Chapter 13

Olivia positioned herself to the side as the last of the mourners filed past through the Harmony Hills gates. She wore a blazer, dark slacks and sunglasses, her hair swept up into a bun. Reilly waited by the hearse. Hands behind his back. Respectful. The air was heavy with the scent of lilies, roses and hyacinths. He wanted to gag. It was cloying.

The service hadn't taken long; the usual prayers said. Niceties passed. Aunt Martha, there was always an Aunt Martha, announced that she'd be hosting a meal and get-together at her house. Vince would have wanted it that way. Amen, move it along.

From behind her dark glasses, Olivia surveyed the headstones, making note of the most recent. One good thing about Harmony Hills, it was large and utilized. People were dying to get in, no pun intended, and that made her work easier.

One of the family, the mother or wife, stopped by Olivia, taking one of her hands in theirs. "It was a lovely service. Thank you for all your help." She looked toward the ground, still clasping Olivia's hand. "He's in a better place."

Olivia smiled a mournful smile and peered over the top of her glasses. "He is."

The woman clucked her tongue and adjusted her pillbox hat, fluffing the black veil. "I must join the rest, I suppose. Thank you, again, dear." She let go and hobbled past Reilly.

Olivia inclined her head toward the woman, and he immediately stepped in, taking her arm and helping her navigate the bumpy ground. Why cemeteries never paved their paths, he didn't know. Once she was safely in her sedan, he made his way back to his station.

The cemetery staff placed the flowers over the grave and removed their tools, then folded the metal chairs. The funeral director made eye contact with Olivia and, walking over, took her by the arm. "It was a lovely service. I am so sorry for your loss."

She patted his hand. "It has been hard."

"If there is anything else you're in need of, please contact me. Whatever I can do." He looked to the horizon where the clouds were darkening. "Yes. If there's anything. Call."

She wiped a non-existent tear and nodded.

He motioned to his men.

Once they were alone, Reilly approached Olivia. "How do you do that?"

"What?" She was now in denim skinny jeans and a black turtleneck, the way she'd met him that morning.

He waved a hand at her, from head to toe. "Change. Like that. You know what I mean."

"Oh." She winked. "Just a little something."

"And the family, they thought you were staff. The workers thought you were family."

"And?"

He fell silent.

"Get the shovel."

Reilly took the shovel from the back of his pickup, more than twenty years old but ran fine. Almost fine. He eyed the rust across its fender, slowly eating the car alive. A losing battle he'd been fighting but, with this job, he should be heading toward a much cushier lifestyle. Perhaps something new would be in his future. Perhaps a lot of new things.

"Yo!"

Olivia's voice brought him out of his thoughts.

"Are you coming, Brutus?" She was standing at the head of the grave, sneakers at the edge of the fresh dirt, arms folded. "Can you stop dreaming for five fucking minutes so we can get a move on?"

"Yes, ma'am." He saluted. It annoyed him that she wouldn't use his name but let it pass. The desire for whatever the hell she touched him with still lingered in his skin. A driving need. She called the shots; his job was to get them done. "What are we after? Jewelry?"

"No, *Reilly*." She spoke as if she read his thoughts. "Bigger things. Much bigger things. Move the flowers and get digging. Vince is waiting."

"Vince." The marker beside the grave read Vincent Palmeri. Reilly piled the flowers to the side and sunk the shovel's blade deep into the earth. It carried with it a damp, musty smell. Fresh. By the time he was coffin-deep, with space around the lid, he was breathing hard.

"Now, what? I didn't bring a pickaxe. Aren't these things locked somehow? To prevent . . . what we're doing?"

"One moment." She closed her eyes and focused, arm outstretched.

Reilly watched as she seemed to emanate a dark aura, as if a black shadow surrounded her. She was shrouded in darkness.

She flipped her hand palm up and he heard the scraping of a latch opening below him.

"Lift the lid."

The logistics weren't the best. It wasn't as if he'd dug standing room around the freaking thing. 'Course digging up coffins hadn't been on his resume. Until now. He pushed enough dirt out of the way to get a foothold beside the end of the wooden box and was able to get his fingers under the lip of the lid. A few good tugs and the hinges turned.

It opened. Reilly scrambled up onto solid ground, away from the stiff before him.

The man couldn't have been more than forty. Dark hair, a few stray grays over his ears. Hands folded across his chest. Dark suit. Probably cost more than all the clothes Reilly owned. Ever.

"What's the treasure?"

"Him."

"Him? We're taking the body?" He was horrified. He'd done a lot of bad things in his life, really bad. Like accidentally killing the guy at the liquor store he was trying to rob. Or at least that was what his lawyer sold the jury. Sometimes things look like what they're not.

"No. The *body* is going to come with us."

"What?" He backed up. "Like get up and walk out of that box?"

"I didn't hire you for your brains, did I?"

"Don't you need like a special knife or something? A book to read from? Candles?"

"What '70s Hammer film do you think this is?"

Olivia climbed into the box with the guy, squatting over his torso as if she was going to give him a final, going away lap dance.

Reilly snickered and she glared at him. "You can be replaced."

She leaned forward, placing one hand over the man's chest; the other gripped his wrist. Her eyes were half shut. The black aura grew, and Olivia swayed, side to side. Side to side. She lifted the man's hand in the air and Reilly caught a glimpse of a small mark on his wrist. A bird.

He absently rubbed the crow that was inked on his own, and an electricity buzzed around them. His tattoo vibrated as Olivia worked. As if they were bound.

Reilly watched as the darkness gained shape, as if thousands of gnawing, buzzing flies engulfed her and the corpse. She was chanting something in a language he hadn't heard before.

The dead man screamed a scream that came from the deepest part of his soul and Reilly staggered backward. The dead man. Screamed. Then everything fell silent. Like a muffled quiet after a snowstorm, before the world went back to living. Even the birds were still. And Reilly was too scared to move.

"Give me a hand." Olivia had her arm in the air, waiting for him to steady her as she climbed to solid ground. She snapped her fingers. "Come on, Brutus. Wake up!"

"I. I," he said, then jerked to reality. He scooped her up beside him.

"You. You." She brushed the dirt off her jeans.

"What did you do?"

"Collected on a debt."

"I don't understand."

"You don't have to." She turned toward the open casket. The man's face, where it had been calm minutes before, looked as if he'd seen his family murdered and was about to be dismembered himself, inch by bloody inch. Fear, terror, wide-eyed horror, was his death mask now. "He sold his soul. Nobody likes when it's time to collect." She sighed. "Cover this up, my man. Make it pretty."

"Sold his soul. Like in the movies." It didn't make sense. That shit was real? He rubbed the back of his neck, feeling the grit and sweat that had accumulated. He kicked the lid shut and started scooping from the dirt pile he'd made.

"Like the movies," Olivia echoed. "But not."

Scoop. Dump. "But when he died, didn't his soul move on to the ether? Go do whatever it is they do, white light and all?" He tipped the shovel and let clumps of dirt slowly fall onto the casket. Dull thuds onto the wood.

"When you desire things you can't get on your own." She put her hands in the air. "Fame. Money. Power." She looked deep into his eyes. "Sex."

A shudder went through him, and heat ran through his groin. He was hard. He wanted her and everything she could give him. Wanted to take her, plow into her with every bit of his being, fuck her on the grave until he was spent, then let her fill him with the power she promised. Whatever he had to do to get it, he would. Without hesitation. He would pimp out his own mother if he had to.

With another snap of her fingers, the feeling was gone. He was empty, hollow. Limp. And she held the reins.

"Do you understand why men sell their souls?"

A quiet yes escaped his lips. A smile curled from hers.

"And would you sell yours?"

The crow that marked him began to burn. A slow heat to an inferno in seconds, enough that he dropped the shovel to the ground and fell to his knees. A sweat broke out across his brow. His tattoo was now a brand.

"You'll get what you want. In time. Now, get to work."

He picked up the shovel and noticed movement beside Olivia. The man from the coffin coalesced before her. Reilly gasped. It wasn't a ghost or hallucination. The man was as solid as he was, but his face was devoid of emotion. Terror mask transformed.

Reilly was rooted to the spot.

"It's not polite to stare." Olivia strode past him and the dead man followed. "Meet me at Forest View over in Freemont when you're done," she said over her shoulder. Then muttered, "Damn, I've really got to change that name." She and the dead man got into her Lexus and exited Harmony Hills.

Reilly followed her orders and contemplated what he'd gotten himself into.

Chapter 14

Dom sat on the sofa in the common room. It was an old thing, duct tape covering rips, stitching frayed at the seams. Overstuffed and showing it. But comfortable, he guessed. If your pants didn't stick to the tape. An old episode of CSI was playing. The guys were always drawn to the cop shows. Definitely not his cup of tea.

Officer Simmons walked in. "Russell, I need you to come with me."

Some whoops went up. "Oh, you're in trouble now!" Dom got up, shaking his head and gave them the finger as he left.

Officer Simmons didn't speak as they walked to a small meeting room. He opened the door, ushered Dom to a seat and took his position outside the door. Two men were already at the table. The first had a buzz cut and was in a yellow polo shirt that almost seemed as overstuffed as the sofa. The sleeves fought to contain the guy's biceps. A weightlifter, with that inspirational bullshit of "I'm here to help YOU help YOURSELF" mentality, or "Buy my protein drink and BUFF UP." He held out his hand and Dom shook it.

"Alan Evans, Director of Hilldale Second Chance. Good to know you, Dominic." His grip was strong, definitive. Top dog and not afraid to say so. He opened a folder from the top of a stack in front of him.

Dom looked to the second man.

"Bob Walters. I've been assigned as your parole officer." The other man stuck out his hand. "We met once years ago."

Met was an understatement. They'd been good friends for a long time and Bob was the one who'd called him to have Out of the

Dark investigate at the prison. A Block, Parker Davies' cell. But he'd play along.

"Mr. Walters. Yes, I think I might remember you."

"Good, good."

"I'll take the lead here, Bob, if you don't mind. I've got another appointment in about," he stared at his watch as if it would announce his schedule to the room, "thirty minutes." He made enthusiastic eye contact with Dom. "To put it in a nutshell, all of your paperwork has been processed. You're set to be released Friday, and you'll be coming to stay at our house."

"Okay."

"I believe Hilldale is your old stomping ground, am I right?"

"I lived there for a few years, yes."

Evans ran a finger down the paper in front of him. "Yes, yes. I see that. Well, I wanted to inform you of the rules of the house, so you're familiar with them before you step foot in the door. Luckily, we had one spot open when they had to reassign you."

He put on a pair of glasses that Dom figured had to be for show and handed him a pale green sheet of paper.

"Now, this is a list of the rules that you can read through. Basically, we require you to maintain sobriety, adhere to an 11:00 p.m. curfew and to sign in and out of the facility, giving us your destination and when you expect to return. There are daily chores to help maintain the house and there are no visitors without prior approval. Cellphone use is restricted to certain times of the day. We find that it's a distraction from what we're trying to achieve." He paused, flipping the page. "We expect you to be actively seeking employment or working toward that end. Respectful conduct, no violence or theft. I believe it's all pretty straight forward."

Dom skimmed the sheet.

"There are also consequences for breaking the rules."

"Naturally." The guy wanted to make him feel like a kid in detention, being read the riot act. Yes, sir. No, sir. Drop and give me twenty. But he'd dealt with demons. He wasn't concerned about a few rules.

"For minor infractions, and we do understand that everyone can make a mistake here and there, there are written warnings. A reminder, but in your house record. If there are multiple infractions, or more serious issues, we have the right to curtail your freedoms or add to your responsibilities within the house. Serious infractions could lead to your discharge from the home, resulting in your return to prison." He paused. "No one wants that, am I right, Dominic?"

"Absolutely right." Canned questions, pat responses.

"In my time with Second Chance, we've never had to discharge anyone. We really want to help our guys get back on their feet and head for success. Do you have any questions?" He leaned back in his chair and placed his glasses on the stack of folders.

"No, I don't think so."

"You'll also have your parole rules and schedule with Mr. Walters here. But he'll go over all of that with you. It's a structured day-to-day life, but it's a good one. And that structure, that routine, we've found, is what sets our guys on the best path. Are you with me?"

"Yes, sure. I guess I am."

"Good man. I'll be there Friday afternoon when you arrive to introduce you to the staff and show you the ropes. Get you settled in. From there, we'll all work together. A big family."

"Family."

"Family. I need you to sign the bottom of that page, showing that you've read and understand the rules and violations. A copy will be given to you when you arrive at the house."

He slid a pen to Dom, clicking the top so it was ready. Dom signed, clicked and shoved both on a return trip across the table to Mr. Inspiration.

"Well," Evans said, gathering his things and tucking the arm of his glasses into the neckline of his shirt. He pulled his jacket off the back of the chair. "It was great meeting you. I'm really looking forward to seeing you on Friday."

He knocked on the safety window of the door and Officer Simmons let him out.

Bob Walters exhaled and smiled at Dom. "Now that that's over, we can get down to real business."

Dom relaxed. A little. "So, you're my parole officer? The last I knew you were a C.O."

Walters shifted, uncrossed his ankles. "After your team investigated Cell 113," he said, "I couldn't work there anymore. It gave me the creeps, the thought of it all."

Dom remembered that night. He'd seen a lot in the years he'd investigated with Out of the Dark, but when the demon slammed through the cell going after Parker Davies . . . Davies, who'd died there but for whatever reason remained after his death . . . it freaked them all out.

"Yeah."

"I put in for a transfer, and then really rethought everything. I eventually switched out of corrections and went into this. Working with guys on their way out works better for me than wallowing in whatever residual shit builds up in that prison. Living or dead. And I'm a year from retiring."

"Congratulations."

Bob leaned his chest into the table and lowered his voice. "I always believed you were innocent, that you were after something evil. I know you were only doing what you needed to. Especially after what we saw that night. It opened my eyes to what's out there." He shuddered, even with it so many years in the past. "Don't let on that we were friends. I wouldn't want the higher ups to squash this assignment on what they deem 'impropriety.' I'm going to do my best for you. Above board and absolutely professional, but I wanted you to know."

"I appreciate that." He wanted to ask where Walters was during his trial. Why he hadn't come forward, said what he'd seen.

Stood up for him. But he knew. He got it. The man would have lost everything, his job, respect in the community, and the outcome would've been the same.

Walters dug through his file on Dom, licking his finger and pulling out specific papers one by one.

"Evans explained the rules for the house, now we get to go over the parole stipulations."

"Fun, fun."

"They're not bad, actually. Logical, rational rules. No alcohol or drugs. Check-ins with me once a week at first. As time goes on, that'll stretch out. No leaving the county or the state. No contact with the victim or the victim's family."

Papers went back and forth between them. Signatures here, initials there. Rules, structure, routine and more rules. He would be "free," but the world would own his ass for a very long time.

"We'll also be talking about your plans for employment."

"Certainly can't go back to teaching."

"Yeah, that would be a hard no."

It came as no surprise. Get put away for second degree attempted murder, with echoes of another murder they can't pin on you, but alluded to, and no college in the world is going to touch that application.

"I'm thinking retirement. Turned sixty-five in this place. Why not? Maybe write a book."

Walters wrinkled his brow, shuffled more papers. "Perhaps. We'll look at all your options. You can apply for social security. I'll get you whatever paperwork you need for that. All in all, you have to be productive, moving forward in a positive way and we'll work on a plan."

"You and Rah Rah Evans."

Walters chuckled. "He is a bit much. But he's not wrong. You'll have to work to get your life back."

And that was exactly what he intended. But he had a plan, he

Barb Shadow

just had to set it in motion.

Chapter 15

Tom dropped his backpack beside his desk. He could hear Paul coming down the hallway, high-fiving and hooting. "Last day of classes, finals week awaits! Woo Hoo!"

"Yo, Rev." The familiar face stuck through his open door. "Wet Raven. 4:00 p.m. Be there." He made finger guns and winked.

"A little early, no?"

"It's 5:00 somewhere."

"Who's the designated?"

Paul raised his eyebrows and inclined his head toward Tom.

"Nope! Not it. I'll come along, but I was it last time."

"Okay, okay. Let me see who I can round up. Be outside at 4:00 and we'll ride together." He stepped into the hallway, leaving Tom's door ajar. "Hey, Mike! Mike, my man!"

Tom opened his laptop. The clock in its corner read 2:57 p.m, so he had a little time. He pulled up his browser and typed Olivia Miranda Mulvey, Aliton. Articles on the trial came up, along with a list of Olivias, Mulveys, and pharmacies. Nothing close to what he was looking for.

He picked up a pen, tapping it against his cheek. What did he know? He had her name, and where she lived more than twenty years ago. He knew she had gone to live with her grandmother out west somewhere after the trial. Seth was her brother. *Foster* brother, he corrected himself. Not any kind of lead there, especially since the guy was dead.

He thought back to the last day he truly remembered spending time with her. Or wanting to. Before the chaos. He'd wandered into her bedroom. She had promised to play with him, and he climbed onto her bed to see what she was doing. Olivia was stuffing things into her survival pack and trying to fit the Ouija board. *His* board. But she was also grabbing money and papers from her desk. Gift cards and things.

Cards!

He got up, shoving his chair behind him, and went to the closet. Sliding the accordion door open, he dug through his things to the back wall where a small box lay hidden inside his suitcase. It was a box of little things, treasures from over the years, that he'd managed to save. It had to be there.

He pulled out a handful of birthday and Christmas cards, dropping a tiny spiderman keychain and some black and orange paperclips. A few sheets of stickers were stuck to some of the other papers, and he had to delicately detach them. Old photos. There were also a few of his drawings and a picture his mother had made for him many years ago. His bio-mother. Folded and tucked away.

Before he could get lost in those memories, he found the envelope at the bottom, wedged into the box. It was red and there were heart stickers across the back. They shone in the light, reflecting little patterns that had always fascinated him. Olivia dropped it when she stuffed everything else into her pack, maybe because she only wanted the money it held, and didn't care about anything else.

It had happened right before the shadow lodged metal darts from the dart board into his leg. He winced at the memory. The *Jetty* shadow. A sadness and an ache of emptiness fought his determination. Jetty had left him. Had hurt him. Jetty, who was a demon and who had taken Olivia.

He pushed the thought aside.

He remembered sitting in Olivia's room after he returned from the hospital, his leg in a cast. Mrs. Resnick saw him turning the envelope over and over, watching the little hearts shine. She let him keep it when he moved to the new foster home. A little something to remember Olivia by. A little something from a happier time.

The card was from Olivia's grandmother.

He prayed as he tucked his fingernail under its edge and tugged it from the box. The hearts still sparkled and, when he flipped it over, the grandmother's address was still legible. 18 Hazel Road, Hartville, Wyoming. Above it, in scratchy handwriting, was her name. Bernice Hendricks.

Thank God! He could have kissed that envelope.

A name, an address. He typed it in. If he could get a phone number, he'd be gold.

Chapter 16

Dom sat on a bench outside of Target while his housemates wandered around inside. He scoffed at the word "housemates." If he wasn't living there as an ex-con himself, he would call it a den of disaster. Most of the guys talked the talk, walked the walk. But only to do their time and get back on the street. Some were already flirting with trouble. Not his problem. He had bigger concerns.

He saw the house van waiting in the parking lot. It felt good to know he was free. Free to sit in the sunshine, albeit chilly. Free to follow the rules that were set for him. But at least he was "on a path." Yeah. If they only knew what path he was on.

Dom set his bag of underwear and socks beside his feet and bent, forearms on his knees, to set up his new phone. A small Tracfone with prepaid minutes. Cheap and easy. Cheap being the biggest plus. He had his bank account, which thankfully had stood the test of time. Time incarcerated, anyway. He had a little money stashed until he figured out his next step. He had to take everything one day at a time.

Once the phone was activated and he confirmed his minutes, Dom pulled a business card out of his wallet. "Parole Officer Robert Walters," he said. "Let's try this thing out."

He dialed.

"Bob Walters."

"Hey, Bob. Dom Russell. How are you this fine day?" He stretched his legs out in front of him and watched a robin hop along the edge of the asphalt lot.

"Dom. I didn't recognize the number that came up on my

console. New phone, I'm assuming?"

"Hell yes." He admired the basic plastic thing in his hands. Basic was right. It could dial a call, maybe send a text. He could even type 5318008 and upside down it would read BOOBIES. All hail what's good and right in the world. Straight up plain.

"It's generally the first thing guys do when they get out, get a phone. You go fancy? Bells and whistles?"

"Nah. I don't need anything like that. Just something that can make a call when I need it."

"Make sure you adhere to their usage rules. They're strict about that."

"No worries," he said. The robin flew as a woman pushed a wagon with two children in tow to her car. "If they check anything, all they'll see is my call to you."

"Good. So, what can I help you with today? Giving me your new number?"

"I need a favor."

He could hear Walters exhale and his chair creak as he leaned away from his desk.

"You know it's way too early to ask for favors. They don't grant shit for the first few months that you're there. They need to see you participate, keep your nose clean, long before they grant you anything extra."

"I get that. I do. But there's something I have to take care of."

"Are you going to tell me what?"

"I'd rather not." He heard the chair snap into position.

"Dom, look," he said, but the man cut him off.

"Here's the deal. It's nothing that will get me in trouble, other than needing to be out of this house for about twenty-four hours."

"Twenty-four. You know that's not pos-"

"I know there're always exceptions and strings that can be pulled. I swear that I won't be anywhere near the kid or her brother. No one will be hurt, and I won't be in a position to get myself arrested." He waited for Walters' reaction. There was none. "I know this is a big one, Bob. I do. And I'm sorry to ask, but I need it. You saw what went on in cell 113. That's only a fraction of what I deal with. A small fraction. And I need to do this. Twenty-four hours and I'm back in my happy little Second Chance home, following every rule like the good boy that I am. I swear."

The line was quiet.

"Trust me."

"I do trust you."

"But?"

"Is this thing you need to do legal?"

"Absolutely. 100%."

"But you won't fill me in."

It was Dom's turn to hesitate. "Plausible deniability. If, in the one in a million chance something goes wrong, and it won't, you have an out."

"An out."

"Are you going to keep repeating everything I say?"

"I might. Till it makes sense." Another exhale that expired into a whistle. "Gimmie some time to think about it. I'll call you back in an hour or two."

"You got it, man. Thank you." He flipped the phone shut and smiled to himself. Bob would do it. He'd come through this time. Being free was good.

Dom stood in front of a cutting board with some tomatoes. It was his rotation of kitchen duties. Cooking, cleanup. Today would be BLTs for lunch and he had the bacon frying on the stove. Jimmy was vacuuming. Raul was working on the lawn. He didn't know where their fourth housemate was. His focus was on the sputtering and spitting of the grease on the stove, and he turned the knob a little lower.

As he sliced through the first juicy tomato, his phone rang. It had been in his pocket since they returned home. Alan had gone through their bags, making sure there was no contraband, and had checked out the phone he'd picked up.

"Do you mind if I take this?" He held up the phone. "Bob Walters."

Evans was stapling some papers to the bulletin board where their chore list, job fair information and house rules were posted.

"Sure, that's fine," he said, Evans picked up the spatula and flipped the bacon. A renewed sizzling filled the room.

"Thanks." Dom walked into his bedroom and shut the door. "Hey, Bob."

"Here's the deal." No warm greeting, no nonsense in his voice. "This is how it's going to go down."

"Okay."

"There's a job fair near Cooperstown next week. It's a little far, but not outside the range of possibilities. I'll let Evans and the powers that be know that I will sign you out, and take you with me, that there are a couple of jobs that would suit you to a T. They should be fine with that and approve it. Once we cross that hurdle, I'll give them a call late in the day that my car broke down, but that we should be back on the road in a couple of hours. You will make your way back ASAP and be in that house before the twenty-four hours are up."

Dom contemplated everything Bob said. "That should work. Tight, but it should work."

"It damn well better."

"Thanks, man. I appreciate this more than you know."

"Yeah, yeah. Just make sure you come back."

"I promise." He crossed his heart and held up two fingers, even though Bob couldn't see. "Scouts honor. Oh, and Bob?" Dom squeezed his eyes shut.

"Yeah?"

"I'm going to need a ride."

Chapter 17

Tom waited in the queue of restless patrons-to-be outside the Wet Raven, cigarette smoke and cheap perfume heavy in the air. The bouncer, a big guy in a black leather jacket, was at the entrance checking IDs. He felt for his wallet, thankful for the familiar bulge in his jacket pocket.

Two steps, pause. Two steps. Tom flashed his ID at the bouncer as he moved with the flow of people into the bar. He'd been there countless times before and they all knew him. Knew he was over twenty-one. Music blared. He stepped to the side, trying to avoid getting jostled by the crowd as he looked for his friends.

But even in the hustle and bustle of the bar, his mind kept going back to Olivia. Like touching a bruise to see if it still hurt. He hadn't been able to find a landline for Granny Bernice, or even a mention of one. Ever. He did make sure there wasn't an obituary for her. But it was strange. Not even a number to try to see if it's disconnected or something. It's like she never owned one, which seemed unlikely, but he figured it was possible.

He was discouraged, at first. But, when life hands you lemons, you go with the next best thing. A visit. A full on, face to face meeting with the woman. Signed, sealed, delivered and booked. He was flying to Hartville, Wyoming, on Wednesday after his last final. He'd find Olivia if it killed him.

Paul caught up with him. "Grab a table, will you?" He was headed toward the bar with their buddy Driscoll. "We'll bring back nachos and a pitcher."

Tom spied a spot in the corner that was free and tipped some chairs around it, taking a seat by the wall. Everyone was out tonight. Classes were over and finals started Monday. He was keyed up. Ready to be done with school. To be on the plane. He wished he could've jumped in his car and started a road trip or been able to book the flight sooner. But he had to get through finals. Graduation was in two weeks.

Except all he could focus on was getting to Olivia.

It was heavy metal night at the Wet Raven, and they had a tribute to Ozzy Osbourne blasting through the house speakers. As Crazy Train began, the bar erupted in, "Ay, ay, ay!" The live band carried in their equipment, setting up on the small stage to his left. J. T. Ripper always put on a good show and Tom nodded to the lead singer as he set a tip bucket beside his music stand.

Paul made it back to the table, bopping to the beat with nachos in hand, with Driscoll carrying the pitcher and glasses. Stephanie slid in beside Tom as Paul started pouring.

"Hey, hey!" she said. "To classes being over!" She held her glass high and clinked with the others. She leaned close to Tom. "And have I got a surprise for you."

"What?"

"I got us in."

"What?"

"I got us in. The Harper house. You know, to investigate." She sat back with a satisfied grin. "It didn't take a lot. The family there was quite into it."

"Seriously?"

"Hell, yes. And you're going with us."

Carly stopped chatting with Paul and looked over. "Did you tell him?" She turned to Tom. "Isn't it great?"

"Well, yeah. I guess it is. When?"

Stephanie took a sip of her beer. "Tonight," she said. "So don't drink too much."

"Tonight. As in tonight."

"The very same. We figured stop by, have a beer or two, grab some dinner and around 10:30 p.m. head to Montgomery. I've got fresh batteries in the voice recorders, and the cameras are charging. Carly's got the K-2. That's really all we need."

"Tonight."

"Got something better to do?"

"No. I don't."

"Good. It'll be fun. At the very least, we'll get to hang out together. At best, we'll pick up some kind of activity. The family didn't report anything out of the ordinary, no bumps in the night to speak of but you never know."

"Sounds good," he said, but he didn't know if it sounded good or not.

Stephanie parked in the driveway at 235 Wilson. She looked up at the house for a minute before shutting off the ignition. The evergreens on the property cast shadows on the home, and the bare branched trees gave more of a Halloween feeling than spring. "Spooky at night, isn't it?" she asked.

"Sure is."

"I love the spooky." She hit the latch release for the trunk. "Let's get started."

Tom joined her at the back of the car as she fished in a bag for her things. Carly pulled up, taking a parking spot on the street.

"There," she said, hanging her camera strap around her neck.

Carly met them at the car. "Nice Victorian. I've always liked the architecture." She walked up the front steps, holding the K-2 in front of her. "Just seeing if there are any odd readings outside."

"I've got the voice recorder on. Make sure you account for the power lines running into the house."

"Noted." Carly was on the porch. She shielded her eyes, trying to see in the picture window. "Are you going to explain this to me? What we're doing and how we're doing it?"

"Every step of the way." They walked up the steps and Stephanie pulled the key out of her pocket. "What Carly has is an EMF detector. When there's a spike in EMF, the lights light up. It means the electromagnetic energy is high."

Carly hit the button on the front of the device, then again, making it light up across its board.

"And that would mean ghosts?"

"Some people think so. A spirit trying to communicate, or manifest."

"Or a refrigerator or other appliance," Stephanie chimed in. "That's one of the reasons we do a walkthrough. To know where energy spikes are with regard to explainable things. Like electrical wiring and such."

"So, a spike apart from those things would indicate a spirit."

"Yes. But we really don't have anything scientific to back it up with regard to the paranormal. But any time we've found something, the K-2 has been pretty accurate," Carly added. "If something spikes and we can explain it, good on us. Better to debunk than get all ghostly gullible."

Stephanie unlocked the door and gave it a small shove. Tom half expected it to open with a creak to a room filled with cobwebs and dust. What they found was a well-furnished, tasteful living room. Sofa under the window to the right, television catty corner. And a white shag carpet.

"Who would ever have a white carpet?" Stephanie asked.

"No one with kids." Tom smiled. "There aren't even footsteps through it."

Tom followed Carly as she continued her sweep of the living room and into the kitchen. Stephanie came up behind him.

"Do you believe in ghosts and spirits? What's the church say?" she asked.

"I know there's more to this life than we realize. I don't know if there are spirits around us or when they move on, but I do believe in heaven and hell. I know there's light and I'm sure there's dark to balance it out. But the church doesn't have a unified stance on it. I'm probably not supposed to be participating in a séance."

"We're not doing a séance."

"Then we're good."

"I figure you'll be our resident skeptic. You know, being almost a priest." She pressed her lips tightly together, her eyes animated.

He took the dishtowel off the faucet and snapped it at her. She jumped out of the way.

Carly finished her sweep. "So far everything's normal. As normal as normal is." She held out the K-2, showing Tom the spike as she moved closer to the refrigerator and then away from it.

"And the voice recorder?" He noticed its red light glowing.

"Always on when we're at a property. You never know when you might catch an EVP, and the best ones seem to pop up when you're not looking for them." Stephanie snapped a few photos.

"EVP?"

"Noob," she joked. "Electronic Voice Phenomenon. Someone speaking who we can't hear at the time, but the recorder catches them."

"Gotcha."

"Never watched Ghost Hunters?" Carly asked.

"Nope."

"Ghost Adventures?"

"Nope again."

"Wow."

Carly left the kitchen, moving on to the bedroom with Stephanie in tow. Tom stood at the basement door. He could hear the girls talking, Carly commenting on how unremarkable the house seemed; Stephanie agreeing that it felt dead as a doornail but that they'd see after they conducted a few EVP sessions.

The door. This was the door. It flashed into his mind. That day. The storm had come out of nowhere, wind blasting through the house. Amanda running. She'd looked up at the window, his mother's art room window, and *seen*. He'd followed her, the voice loud in his mind. Telling him what to do. Telling him not to stop. Find her. Kill her. He'd picked up a shard from the mirror that had shattered in the living room and matched her step for step as she backed down her stairs. Watched her fall.

He couldn't go down there. Couldn't face the final memory that was waiting to pierce his brain. Panic grew in his chest. He knew he should breathe but his lungs couldn't fight past the hold this memory had on him. Inhale. Exhale.

Let it go.

But it dogged him. He saw it. He knew it. At only five, how could he have physically killed a grown woman? His hands were shaking. Heart like a sledgehammer in his chest. He'd done it, though. And here they were, searching for spirits.

One spirit. Amanda.

What if they found her? What if she was there because she couldn't move on because of what he'd done? What Black had done through him. Could she forgive? Would she?

He prayed, harder and faster than he ever had before. For Amanda's soul. For his own.

His thoughts were flying faster than his heart could race and he jumped when Stephanie touched his arm.

"Whoa, big fella. Lost in thought or what?"

Carly's hand was on the doorknob.

Shake it off. Shake it off. He took a deep breath.

"You okay?"

"Fine. Yeah, fine. Got hit by some memories of my childhood."

"Must've been doozies," Carly said as she swung open the door and started down the steps. "Who's up for the basement?"

"Not me."

Stephanie furrowed her brow. "You sure you're okay? Is this creeping you out? Because if it is, we can stop."

"No, no. Go ahead. That's where Amanda Harper was murdered and I think I'd rather stay up here for now. You go. Really."

She didn't look convinced. "Okay."

"You coming?" Carly's voice came from below. Muffled.

"On my way. I think we need to do an EVP session down there. Tom says that's where the woman was killed."

Tom went into the kitchen and splashed water onto his face. He dried his hands on the dishtowel, then his cheeks. It smelled faintly of Dawn dishwash and mold. Not everyone thought to wash their rags. He switched on the light over the sink. It didn't need to be dark. If there were spirits around, they'd be there night or day. Taking a seat at the dinner table, he admired the room. It was painted pale yellow, light and welcoming. He could hear the girls' voices and tried not to think about Amanda.

"Amanda, are you here with us tonight?"

"If you come close to this little box, it will let us know you're here by lighting up."

"We don't want to hurt you. We only want to talk with you. Acknowledge your presence here."

"Do you know who murdered you?"

Tom's heart stopped and his throat tightened. What if she answered? Would he be tried for murder? Maybe he should be. No one would believe it. Or would it be yet another "dark entity defense"?

Parker Davies. Dominic Russell. Him.

But he wouldn't relive that memory. He'd tamp it down so hard nothing would ever trigger it. He'd force it into a box, lock it and throw away the key. And next he'd find Olivia. He'd get answers and then he'd go after the demon that did this. This was his mission. His calling.

He got up from the table and found a window where he could see next door. His old house. The moon gave a little light. He stared up at the art room window, trying to make sense of the shadows. Willing the tree limbs to quit swaying so the shadows would be still.

Squinting, he was sure he could make out the likeness of his mother. The face he'd seen in pictures kept safe in his box of treasures. He peered at her, what he thought must be her, and then she was gone. But why would she be there instead of moving on? Why hadn't she let go of this life and gone to live with God?

Because of him? The demon?

Tom touched the glass, cool under his fingertips, and held his breath. Waited for her to return to the window. Nothing. Maybe it had been the tree shadows. He didn't believe it. It had to be her.

He'd bought a ticket for Ozzy's Crazy Train and none of this was making sense.

Chapter 18

Reilly packed the dirt around Margaret Finnegan's grave as Olivia walked with the dead woman to his truck. She decided that the newly deceased, as clean as they may appear, were not fresh enough to ride the half hour from Montgomery to Freemont in her car. Warming days and embalming fluid do that. And decomposition, slowed but ever present. 'Course now, he didn't know what to expect from these things. Did they follow Olivia forever? Did they have an expiration date? Fuck all, she was raising the *dead*.

As he drove, he was careful to keep his elbow as close to his ribs as possible. With Margaret between them, he couldn't stomach thought of touching the cool flesh beside him. Once, when he shifted gears, his hand brushed against her knee. A small flap of skin rose up, revealing a writhing gray mass underneath. He nearly puked.

"Turn left up ahead."

"Thought you wanted the highway. Get Mrs. Finnegan here to Forest View." Maybe if he used their names, the bile wouldn't rise so high in his throat. Pretend they were alive. Fake it till you make it. His tongue tasted like his breakfast had gone acid.

"Take it. There's something else we need to attend to."

"Sure." He hated when she was demanding, which was always. There was an energy that bled off her. And off the apartment building. It was thick in that place. Made his hair stand on end sometimes.

"Park here. This block."

He swung the pickup into a space in front of Lather Up, a baseball themed hair salon. Too cutesy for his liking. Not that he ever used a salon. He could shave his own head. Cut his own toenails.

"Margaret, stay here," Olivia commanded.

"Yes, ma'am." Margaret's brown eyes were dull, cataract faded. Her face, expressionless.

"Reilly, you're with me."

"What are we doing? Do I need to bring anything?"

"If we needed anything, Brutus, I would have told you. Bring yourself. Just don't be obvious."

Olivia headed down the street, looking back once to be certain that Margaret remained where she was told.

"Yes, ma'am." Reilly mimicked the dead woman.

Olivia choked back a laugh. "Come on. We don't have a lot of time."

He stole a look at his watch. 11:35 p.m. Not that he had anywhere to go. This was his full-time gig, at the beck and call of little miss witch. Correction. *Necromancer.* He didn't believe she was either, really. Just a chick who found a way to latch onto the teat of power.

On Wilson, she ducked down the side alley between it and the fence of 231, then circled to the back. Reilly followed, glancing to each side, making sure no one was watching. The woman in 231 had the television up loud enough he didn't have to see it to know what show was on. I Love Lucy. The grapes episode. Classic.

Olivia stood at the back door to the house. "Open it."

"You want me to break in."

"Why do you always question, and repeat, what I tell you? Yes. I want you to break in. Without anyone hearing or wondering what the hell is going on. Yes. Please do." She stepped aside, hands on her hips. Exasperated.

"Okay, okay. They'll hear you before they hear me." He examined the door. Simple. The knob was cheap and old. Just needed to pop the lock. He reached into the pocket of his denim jacket and removed a small screwdriver.

"You carry a screwdriver in your jacket?"

"Since working for you." He inserted it, wiggled it and click. It sprung open.

Olivia walked inside. The dust was thick, and cobwebs hung from every corner. It made the kitchen dull and uninviting. Unlived in. That happens when you hang yourself upstairs. No one wants that energy in their home. Or that Harper woman's murder next door. Just as well. It would make everything much easier.

"Do you want me to?" He motioned inside, outside.

"Yes, yes. Come along. No one heard us and, believe me, no one will see us. This shouldn't take long." She walked to the staircase. "When we get where we're going, there'll be paintings along the walls. You need to find me the one of the Ouija board. Set it somewhere flat and put this," she pulled a quarter out of her pocket, "at the center. When I signal, you'll slide it to hello and leave it there."

A curt nod.

They walked together up the steps, past the landing, and stopped when it opened to a large room to their left and a hallway. Reilly noticed that none of the doorknobs matched.

Ahead of them, a door closed.

"Someone's here," he whispered, putting himself in front of her. It was instinct, and he kicked himself for it. He wasn't paid to be a bodyguard, and God knew the woman could take care of herself.

"Don't worry. I've got this," she said. "Lilith? Is that you?"

Silence.

"I'm not here to harm you. Not at all. I want to help."

"Who's Lilith?" Reilly whispered.

"Shut the hell up. I'm working."

He backed off. If she was working, then whatever shut that door wasn't living. His hackles went up, goosebumps prickling along his arms. This stuff always freaked him out.

"Lilith." Olivia's voice took on a singsong, soft quality as she walked farther down the hallway, her footsteps swallowed by the thick carpeting. Everything felt muted and a little cold. "Lilith, I want to help. You died terribly and I know you miss your little boy. Isn't that right? Tommy? I know it's been a long time, but I know you remember."

A sob, feminine and heartbroken, emanated from the next room.

Reilly shuddered.

"Lilith, I understand. And I can help you get to Tommy. I can bring the two of you together once more. You can hold him. Be with him. Forever." Olivia rested her hand on the crystal knob. "Can I open this door? You can trust me. I communicate with spirits and help them cross over to their loved ones."

He smirked. A different story, a new illusion, for everything she touched. God, he wanted that. And she knew it. Since that first kiss, he hungered for the gifts she had.

"I have a friend with me, just so you know. I'm not alone. He's my security. A protector. A girl can't be too careful. The world can be a scary place, especially when you're alone. Let me help you, Lilith. Let me reunite you with your son."

The lock clicked and unlatched. She stepped into the room. Reilly entered behind her and began looking for the painting.

"Thank you." She stepped into the room. "My name's Olivia and that," she pointed at her partner, "is Reilly."

He paused his search to sneeze. "Uh, hello."

There were fewer paintings than Olivia had pictured. The room was in disarray. "They came for your things, didn't they?" She caught some motion out of the corner of her eye, toward a corner in the shadows. A shift in energy. "I bet that made you angry. They had no right to come into your house, your personal space and start taking things. And right after your tragedy. Your life stolen. Your son." Olivia shook her head. "I lived in the house they brought him to. We played together."

My son

Olivia felt more than heard the words. As if Lilith reached out and touched her mind. "Yes. Your little Tommy. He misses you horribly."

Tom Tom

The spirit was closer now, clinging to Olivia's words. Letting her guard down. Reilly placed the painting of the Ouija board on a small desk near Olivia and rested the quarter in the middle.

You can help

"I can. You can be reunited with Tommy. Hold him in your arms. Just take my hand."

Lilith moved forward, a flowing wisp of spirit, coalescing as she glided to Olivia. Her hair cascaded to her shoulders as the colors of her dress grew less opaque. She reached for Olivia's outstretched hand. They connected.

"Now, Reilly."

He slid the quarter to hello and stood transfixed at what he was witnessing.

Olivia closed her hand around Lilith's fingers, gripping them as a black band encircled both, tightening. Lilith's eyes went wide. She fought to get away, her body contorting and twisting, but unable to release the grasp.

Black's energy surged, fueling the portal open. The intensity of its momentum grew like a tornado of darkness as Lilith was drawn in. She loosed a blood curdling scream as the swirling evil tore her apart and sucked her through the gateway.

All went silent as the dust settled.

Reilly held his breath, unblinking.

"Destroy the painting and let's go. Before they get here."

"What did you do?" He stared at the board, unable to take his eyes off the thing. Unwilling to touch it.

"Took out a little insurance. Get your ass in gear. He'll be here soon."

"What? Who?" His legs felt like sandbags in cement.

"Santa Claus. Painting destroyed, us out. Now, Brutus, or you're fucking next." She whirled on her heel and went out the door.

Reilly picked up the painting and put his fist through it, then ran after Olivia.

Chapter 19

The girls returned from the basement. Tom was still at the window, his eyes unwavering from the next house. Wanting to believe it was the shadow of a tree branch. Knowing he'd witnessed something more.

"How'd it go down there?" he asked. Balancing on a highwire with that question, too. He wasn't sure he wanted to hear what they'd experienced. And that came with guilt. He should be better than this. He was mortal. A sinner. But he was also a man of God.

"Nothing out of the ordinary that we could tell," Stephanie offered. "Took a bunch of pictures, tried for EVPs. Next is a session up here." She set the camera on the sofa and stretched.

He tapped on the window. "I want us to go there."

Stephanie walked over to what see he was pointing at. "Your old house?" She peered at the house, unsure what in particular caught his interest.

"Yeah."

"I can see if I can get permission. Maybe line it up."

"No. I want to go tonight."

"We can't barge in somewhere without getting it okayed first. Not only is it trespassing, it's breaking and entering. No one lives there, Tom. We could get in a lot of trouble."

"Yeah, not a good idea," Carly added. "There goes the reputation of our team."

"Your two-person team." Tom needed to get into that house tonight. Needed to prove to himself that he wasn't crazy. That he'd seen his mother. But then what? Was she actually there or was he losing his mind? Maybe he was so caught up in everything that he was hallucinating, or at the very least suggestible.

"A team's a team. We run on our reputation."

He dropped his hands to his sides. "I get that. I do. Is there anything I can say that would get us in there tonight?"

Carly shook her head as she switched out the battery on the camera for a fresh one.

"What have you got?" Stephanie asked. "Go for it."

"Steph!"

"I saw my mother." He swallowed, went back to the window and pointed up toward the second floor. "I saw my mother standing in her art room."

Both girls were at the window now. Carly snapped the battery compartment shut and let the camera whir to life while she craned to see.

"Which one? Left or right?"

"The second one. Right."

They crammed together, staring. Carly shined a flashlight up into the room. "Can't see anything at this angle."

Tom was the first to pull away. "I'm going to check it out. You two don't have to come if you don't want to. No problem. But I'm going over there."

Stephanie grabbed his arm. "We can get some photos outside. Some different angles. See if we can catch what you saw."

He nodded, raising his eyebrows. "That's great. You do that. Meanwhile, I'm going around back to see about finding a way in."

Tom strode out the front door without stopping, Stephanie at his heels. Carly took her time, taking pictures as she went. Attempting to capture the house from different vantage points, with an eye on the side window. She wedged her back against the Harper house, feet on a mound of frozen mud.

Stephanie caught up with Tom as he rounded the corner to the backyard. "Tom, you can't." She brushed the hair out of her face. "I get that you're excited. We're all in when we catch some good evidence. But."

"Evidence?" He spun toward her, his voice tense but controlled. "You've got it wrong. This is my mother. My *mom*. This goes a little deeper than wanting to catch a ghost."

"Hey." She held up her hands. "I'm sorry. I didn't mean how it sounded. Really."

He took a breath. "I know. I just have to check this out. I have to see if she's there."

She gave in with a nod and went with him to the back door. He felt along the doorframe, then turned the knob. It opened in his hand.

"It's been jimmied."

"What? How can you tell?"

"Give me your flashlight."

Stephanie dug into her pocket and brought out a small keychain. Turning a crank on the side of the little light, she slid its button on and handed it to him.

"Look. See how there're little digs in the wood here? Right above the knob? And watch." He shook the knob, turning it left and right. "The lock doesn't catch. Someone was here."

"It's been sitting empty for so long, probably a lot of kids have broken in over the years. With its history . . ." She stopped.

"It's okay." He squeezed her hand. "Its history happens to be my history. But ancient." He sighed, handing back the flashlight. "You and Carly waiting out here? Warming up the getaway cars or what?"

Carly peeked around the corner at them. "I am. In fact, I'm leaving. No offense, guys. I've got a scholarship and two semesters left till I graduate. Not going to risk it."

"That's cool," Tom said. "No offense taken. Let me know what you get from next door, okay?"

"You got it." She snapped the lens cover on her camera and headed toward the street and her car.

"Night, Carl." Stephanie stuffed her hands in the pockets of her jacket and shivered. "Well?"

"Well?"

"It's cold out here and you'll need the voice recorder. Are we going in or what?" She pushed its on button. The little red light glowed.

He smiled. "You bet."

The entryway led them through a small mudroom and into the kitchen. Tom rested his hand on the counter, grimaced at the slick feeling of dust, and sneezed.

"Bless you."

The garden window and sliding doors to the patio let in the moonlight, helping them navigate to the living room.

"Does it look familiar? Do you recognize the place?"

He stood in the middle of the empty room, turning, turning. "There was the picture of a bird on this wall. A big black bird. Crow, I'd guess. Nothing else really stands out to me."

"Bare walls and no furniture probably make it feel entirely different."

"Yeah. Let's go upstairs. Didn't the old woman say they'd left in the middle of packing the place up?"

They started up the carpeted steps. Tom paused at the landing to touch the wall. "Mom hung my drawings here." His hand brushed a plastic frame he hadn't seen in the darkness. "Still got that light?"

She wound it and handed it over.

Hanging on the wall was one of his childhood drawings. A stick figure woman with a black, amorphous blob beside her. He ran his finger across the glass.

"Wow," she said. "What's that?"

"Mom. And our . . . cat." The word stuck in his throat, didn't want to cross his tongue. Cat. Their *cat* Jetty. Their cat but not a cat.

The thing that befriended him when he was young and alone. His blood went cold. He didn't know what waited for him upstairs or if it had been truly his mother in the window. Panic set in. "You," he said, licking his lips with a tongue that was suddenly bone dry. "You need to go wait in the car."

"Why? Tom, I'm not leaving. That's ridiculous."

"There are things I haven't mentioned to you. Memories that have been resurfacing. A lot of bad things went on in this house. Really bad. Dark. I don't want you involved if any of that is still here."

"Then you shouldn't be alone, either."

"Maybe not." He looked up the rest of the stairs. To the left, it opened to a playroom. The hallway held four other rooms. His old bedroom, his mother's, the bathroom and the art room. He was five again, running from door to door. Hearing his mother call to him. *Thomas Ethan, come brush your teeth.* Giggling as he hid from her in his footie pajamas. Running into her arms.

A glint of moonlight shone across the hallway. The art room door was open. His desire to see his mother's spirit transformed into trepidation. He'd wanted this. Needed it. Forced them to break into a house, or at least step inside one already violated.

He pushed onward. One foot, the other. Hand on the railing. In his peripheral vision, he saw toys cars in the open room. An ache filled his heart, expanding into his chest. Sadness gripped his throat. At the top of the stairs, Stephanie put her hand on his shoulder.

"If she's here, we'll find her."

Another lick of his lips. "Yeah."

The footprints in the old, dusty carpet were evident. A disturbance they could make out with only the moonlight as their guide, and they weren't those of kids looking for a place to smoke weed or throw some graffiti up on the walls. They made a path directly to the art room. Trespassers with a purpose. Direction.

With his left arm, Tom put Stephanie behind him. He was no fighter, but if someone was there, he wouldn't have her surprised first.

He'd be the distraction so she could run.

They reached the doorway and Tom instinctively reached inside to hit the light switch. He clicked it up and down, then realized there wouldn't be any electricity. "Hello? Anyone here?"

No movement, no sound. The air in the room was stale and held a faint odor of chemicals. The paint and whatever his mother had used to clean brushes. It smelled like home.

Tom stepped in first, using Stephanie's keychain light. Paintings of broken porcelain dolls filled the walls, with canvases stacked off to the side. No interloper. No burglar, teenager or madman. He exhaled. "Whoever was here must've gone. Maybe today, maybe days ago. I don't know. At least they're not here now."

Stephanie stared at the artwork. "Wow." A painting caught her attention, pulled her in. The doll could have been real. Its face was delicately perfect with half of its skull sunken in, broken, one eye permanently shut. She blew on the canvas, some of the dust flying but most of it thick and clinging to the artwork. "Your mom was an amazing artist," she said. "And rather creepy, if you don't mind me saying so."

"Yeah." He went to the window, standing where his mother must have stood. Where she'd been not long before they arrived.

"Whoa."

"What?"

"Check this out." Stephanie picked up a painting that had been tossed to the side. "A Ouija board, but it's got a hole like someone put their fist through it."

Tom took it from her and held it in front of the window. "Kids. Must've been kids." He propped it against the wall.

"I don't think so. Too deliberate. And why just the one? Something weird there."

He agreed. It was strange.

"Are you ready to start?" She held up the voice recorder, still running.

"Sure. Go ahead."

Stephanie moved around the room, admiring the paintings. "Is there anyone here with us?" Pause. "Mrs. Anderson?"

Tom cleared his throat. "Her name was Lilith."

"Lilith, are you here? My name is Stephanie. Your son Tom is here. He thought he saw you at the window."

They waited between questions. A respectful pause in case his mother wanted to answer. Tried to communicate.

"We don't want to upset or bother you in any way. We only want to make contact; let you know that Tom is okay. A fine grown man. A lot of time has passed, and we want you to know it's okay to cross over. You don't need to stay in this place."

"Please, Mom." His hands were shaking. Hoping for something but didn't know what. A word, a phrase, a touch on his shoulder. A spectral hug. Or that she left long ago and it was his mind playing tricks on him. But Jet was involved. He mentally shook off that thought. Black was involved. A demon.

"If you speak next to this recorder," Stephanie held it up, then set it on the windowsill, "we'll be able to play it later and hear your voice."

Twenty minutes went by. Half an hour.

Tom put his arm around Stephanie's shoulders. "We should probably get out of here."

"Are you sure?"

"Weren't you the one who didn't want to come in the first place?" he asked. "Now you want to move in?"

She smiled. "I only meant if you were ready."

"I am. I haven't seen or felt anything unusual. Not that I'd know if a ghost was standing beside me blowing in my ear. But I'm ready to head home."

Stephanie agreed and they made their way out.

Chapter 20

Tom roused early that morning, throwing on sweatpants and a heavy sweatshirt. His sneakers were laced, and he was out the door before the dorm woke. It was a grey morning, misty. The plowed up dirty snow piles were shrinking, becoming small mounds of their former grandeur. He walked, hands deep in the kangaroo pocket of his shirt. This was what he needed. Some time alone to think.

He was sure he'd seen his mother. Sure as he knew his own name. And the horrible things that were clawing their way into the forefront of his mind . . . Amanda. Her death *at his hands*. He didn't know how to reconcile that. The death of his mother. Demons. Until recently, they'd only been articles on a computer screen, and he wasn't even certain what had triggered his searches. One keyword led to another and there he was.

For a long time he walked, blankly, numb to any thought. Only taking in the smell of the wet snow and the dampness of the fog on his face.

He stumbled, his sneaker gliding over a pebble. He'd walked the perimeter of the campus, past the dorms. The classroom buildings. The gym. The lights were on, and a couple of guys were using the machines. It wasn't for him. He'd never been an exercising kind of person. Didn't have the motivation. Walking was more his forte. He kept on until he'd made the full loop and found himself in the quad. The fountains were coming on. He chose a bench and sat, slouched. Legs stretched out in front of him, ankles crossed.

The sun moved a little higher in the sky and the fog was burning off. Here he was at the Dansville School of Divinity, graduating and receiving his degree as a minister in less than two weeks, and he didn't know what to believe. He didn't understand how to rectify all that'd been throwing itself at him. He knew he had to find Olivia. Maybe his answers would lie with her. Maybe he'd find more questions.

"Contemplating your performance on my final tomorrow?"

Tom sat up. "Dr. Peters. Good morning."

The man before him, clerical collar, dark overcoat, held a Dunkin' bag in one hand and a coffee in the other. He had on a black trapper hat with the ear flaps down.

"I had a chance to read through your paper."

"Oh?"

Peters popped open the lid of his coffee and held the cup to his nose, breathing in the aroma. "Yes." He took a sip. "A fair amount of fluff, but the bare bones were solid."

"Thank you."

"Next time, no fluff. Even if a paper is brief, if you hit the intended points, you will fulfill the obligation you were given."

"Yes, sir."

The man paused, taking another sip of his hot coffee. "Have you had breakfast?"

"No, sir. Not yet."

"Well, Tom, it's after 10:30. You'll be hitting lunch soon. Come. I'm on my way to the office. Let's get warm and you can have a blueberry muffin. I pick up a few because I always find students hungry when they come to see me. I don't eat them myself." He made a fist and tapped his chest. "Heartburn. I had a breakfast sandwich."

"Oh, thank you, but I-"

"Tom, you'll find in this life that a man's day runs better if he has breakfast. The thoughts flow easier, physical work is more pleasant and you'll be on your game. People will listen when you speak." He bent forward. "And besides, you look like you need someone to talk to."

Maybe he did. "Thank you."

They walked along the damp pavement listening to the birds.

They stepped inside the small room and Tom waited while Peters hung his coat on the coat tree in the corner. Bookshelves lined the walls, except where the man's diplomas and certificates were hanging. Master of Ministry, Doctor of Ministry in Applied Leadership, and a few Tom couldn't read from where he stood. Peters secured his hat on a hook and sat in the leather chair behind his desk. The room smelled of old books and prestige.

"Blueberry muffin?" He opened the bag.

Tom took it and the napkin that were offered and sat in an easy chair angled toward his professor's desk.

"Water?" The man turned toward a mini fridge located behind his desk. "I'm sorry there's not something else. I tend to forget to stay hydrated and stock up when they're on sale."

"That would be great. Thanks."

Peters put a stack of papers in front of Tom on the edge of the desk. "No coasters," he said. "But you can use these."

Tom bit the muffin, crumbs falling into his lap, and put the water bottle on the desk.

The professor settled in, dropping his coffee lid into the trash. He held the cup with both hands, elbows on his armrests, and looked at Tom. "Eat first. Then we'll talk."

Tom took another bite and nodded. Dr. Peters had been his favorite professor over the years at Dansville and he appreciated the man's interest. In class, he was strict. Authoritarian. But if you followed his rules, followed his example, he'd give you a glimpse of the caring person behind it all. The man was an icon at seminary and students clamored for his courses. Some regretted it. His grading was tough. Course material rigorous. But Tom had thrived on the man's lectures.

He was a vivid storyteller and had made the Bible come to life. His history classes made you feel as if you were living at the time of Christ. He hoped the man would be able to give him some clarity.

For a few minutes, Peters enjoyed his morning coffee. Light and sweet. Tom finished the blueberry muffin, savoring the crunchy coating of sugar on top. Peters smiled when he went for the water, holding up his cup in mock celebration.

"To hydration."

"To hydration."

"Good. Something we agree on. It's always nice to begin on common ground."

"Always."

"So, why such a glum look out on the compound? Finals related, employment trepidation? Love life?"

"None of the above."

"Oh?"

Tom shook his head. "I need some guidance with regard to where we stand on demons, possession and the like."

Peters raised an eyebrow, but didn't act surprised, as if he'd faced this question multiple times over the years. The man ran a hand across his face and up over the bald top of his head. White hair clipped short against the sides added to his sage visage. He thought for a moment before speaking.

"Moreso than what we've touched on in your classes."

"Yes, sir."

"Well, let's start with that and then see where we springboard, all right?"

"Please."

"Fine." He placed his cup on a separate stack of papers to his right. "You know, as the Bible teaches us, God is in absolute control. Christ defeated Satan and believers in Christ are protected by God's sovereign authority. I know that's incredibly brief and is a simple summation. It encompasses all time. You need something more directly applicable to today.”

“Yes.”

“The church itself varies from parish to parish, minister to minister. The core beliefs remain, but often times subjects such as this, on the peripheral of our main teachings, can vary greatly. I can give you my take on it and we’ll see if I can answer whatever questions are nagging you.” He took a mouthful of coffee, wiped the bottom of the cup with a tissue, and returned it to its paper-stack coaster.

“1st Thessalonians 5:5 tells us that we are children of the light, not the darkness. Do I believe there are demons? Sure. I don’t think about it much as since I’m a believer in Christ, they have no foothold. I don’t believe they’re hanging around on the Earth trying to push people into wrongdoing. As for possession, I suppose it could be possible, but I don’t put much stock in it.”

“No?”

“Not really. I think most cases that are reported as possession or oppression are more of a metaphor for destructive issues like compulsive behaviors or addiction. Fear, maybe. If you look throughout our history, people in times past thought that an epileptic fit was possession by the devil. Or those with intellectual disabilities. They were feared. Put into institutions. It wasn’t something understood, and everyone thought demons were to blame. As we evolve and learn more about the human brain, many of these past quote-unquote possessions are explained. To me, most recent discussions on possession are sensationalized.”

Tom wiped his mouth with the napkin and tossed it into the trash.

“People have always thrown the blame of things they couldn’t understand onto demons. If their lives were unraveling. A lost job, crops failing, the loss of a loved one. All of the above at once.” He picked up his coffee. “Something had to be blamed. And, if the person was mentally ill, well, there you go. Remember, they used to drill holes in people’s skulls to ‘let the demons out.’ They also used possession as an excuse."

"How so?"

He smiled. "Before your time. Back in the 1970s, there was an expression made popular by a television show. The Flip Wilson show, if I remember correctly. That expression was 'The Devil Made Me Do It.' Now suppose you went out and sinned. Committed adultery, for example. You knew it was wrong, and you got caught. Well, you'd save face if you could blame it on the devil or one of his minions and you weren't in your right mind. Look at the Salem witch trials. How many girls lied about their neighbors?"

"True."

"But I'm all over the place. We need to narrow our focus to what's been on your mind."

"I'm really unsure how to frame it."

"Begin at the beginning. What's nagging you?" Peters remained silent, waiting for Tom to gather his thoughts.

"When I was little, no more than five years old, my mother supposedly killed herself and," he swallowed, his mouth dry at sharing anything regarding Amanda, "that same weekend, my neighbor was murdered."

"I'm very sorry to hear that, Tom. My condolences. It must have been a very hard time."

"Thank you. I don't remember much about it, or I didn't. Lately I've been having a lot of old memories resurface. Like I'm finally able to remember things from then. But they're very dark. I had an imaginary friend."

"That's very common, especially in children who experience trauma."

"It was prior to the trauma. From what I'm seeing, what's hitting me, is that he was a demon and caused the tragedies."

"I see."

"I was placed in foster care and lived with a family for a couple of months. I believe at that time the demon left me and began influencing my foster sister. It wasn't long afterward that the older boy in the house was murdered. I've been trying to locate my foster sister to find out what she remembers. Or has lived through. I believe she may have been possessed. May still be."

"Hm. Well, you've put your concerns into quite a nutshell, as well."

"Yes."

"Have you ever been to therapy? Any sort of counseling for all the tragedy you experienced at such a young age?"

"No, I haven't. Or maybe I did, when I was younger. I really don't remember. But nothing in many years."

"It seems to me that you have a lot of unresolved issues resulting from it all. Obviously, with memories coming to light, it would be useful to have someone trained in that area to discuss it all with. Someone who could sort through it and give you the correct tools to deal with them."

Therapy. Logical answer, not what he was looking for. Not what he'd asked. Yes, therapy would help but it wouldn't solve anything. It wouldn't tell him if there was a demon or if Olivia was still possessed. Or what he could do about it.

"I will think about that." He might. Later on, if things didn't change. If worse things surfaced. But he had bigger issues on his plate. Greater fish to fry. His mental state was the least of it all.

"Good. Keep in mind that under hypnosis, people have talked about early memories that later proved to be false. The trauma may have given birth to some false memories that keep you off the track of your real ones because they are too painful."

"I believe my pull to the ministry was because of my past, even though I didn't know it."

"Are you struggling with your calling?"

"Oh, no. Not at all. I'm very happy with it and think it'll be fulfilling."

"Also good. But know it's natural to question. Everything.

Different points in your life will bring you to introspection."

"Yes, sir."

The secretary knocked and peeked in. "Your 11:15 appointment is here, Dr. Peters."

"Thank you. I'll be done in a few minutes."

She closed the door after her.

"So, what do you think, Tom? Is there anything else you'd like to cover before we wrap things up?"

Tom picked up the water bottle as he stood. "What do you think of ghost hunting?"

The man inhaled, pulling his thoughts together. "Another nutshell." He smiled. "I think it's reckless. Risky. Dangerous, perhaps. The church doesn't believe in ghosts. Why would they linger? They either move on or are separated from God. The Bible warns against trying to speak with those who have died. Warns against dealing with mediums. You're inviting negative energy or entities into your life."

"I visited my old house, from when I was five. Before my mother died. I could have sworn I saw her standing in an upper window."

"I see. Perhaps a shadow? Maybe a hallucination due to these memories showing up?"

"Maybe." He didn't believe that in the least. He knew what he saw. Who.

"I have a card here of a good counselor." Peters leaned forward and thumbed through a rolodex on his desk. "Old fashioned, I know. But my mother always said, 'If it ain't broke, don't fix it.'" He laughed and held out a business card.

Tom took it. After a glance, he shoved it into his kangaroo pocket.

"He's a good guy and can help you put those pieces together. Like I said."

"Yes, sir."

"It was a good talk. I hope I helped on some level. Even if it was just to point you toward the therapy. I do feel it will help, Tom."

"I appreciate your time, Dr. Peters." He held out his hand, and the man shook it.

Tom left.

Peters pushed the button on his intercom to let his secretary know he was ready for the next student. He did hope that Tom would get help. He was such a fine young man to be having mental issues.

Chapter 21

Reilly walked back and forth in his apartment, jaw set. Number 104, first floor. Didn't know why it started in the hundreds when he was off the main hallway. It should be number four. Pace. From his front door to the sliding doors that opened to a small porch. Back again. His muttering became talking. To himself. To the walls.

It twisted his brain when Olivia reanimated Vince; his mind was still reeling. But damn. What she did with that poor woman who wanted her little boy. His thoughts drifted to his own mother. A single mom with three kids. She would have done anything to make sure they were okay, just like this Lilith woman. She was only searching for her little boy.

And Olivia tricked her. Tortured her. He didn't understand why. What could this woman have done that deserved being torn apart after death? He didn't think he could go on with this. Didn't know if he could be a part of whatever the grand scheme was. The big picture looked bleak and static filled.

He knew there were ghosts. Had seen his fair share of shit over the years, particularly in Aarondale Correctional. Parker died in 113, but when the COs tried to sell it as a suicide, hah! They all knew it was something dark, a demon, whatever you wanted to call it. They knew. He knew Parker and that guy never would have offed himself.

But this was some next level shit. He could handle the ghost stuff. Even deal with her raising the dead, he guessed. Amass her servants. Grow the fucking Cult of Olivia, if she wanted. He could keep his distance, walk the opposite side of the hallway if they were there. Whatever. They'd all fizzle out at some point, like little bunnies without Energizers. But tearing up souls. *Souls.*

What was it his grandmother said? *The only thing you truly own in this world is your soul. Everything else can be taken away. Stolen, lost, trashed. Your soul remains.* He wasn't a religious man. Not a church goer. Never really thought about any of it. But Grandma imparted some truths into his head that didn't make sense till now. And what was he going to do about it?

There were two choices. Roll with it or quit. And he didn't think quitting was an option.

He had to talk with Olivia. Had to get some answers. And he needed to find a way to protect himself.

Chapter 22

Paul sat on Tom's bed, tossing a crumpled paper ball into the air and catching it. "Tell me again what you're doing and why." He threw it against the poster at the foot of the bed, a sunrise with Proverbs 3:5-6 written across it in flowing script. *Trust in the Lord with all your heart.* The ball hit *heart* and rebounded against the side wall.

Tom finished folding a black tee shirt and added it to a small stack of clothes. A pair of jeans, some socks. Underwear. "I'm packing to catch a flight to Wyoming."

"And why?"

"Olivia's grandmother doesn't have a phone."

"And . . ."

"I need to find my foster sister."

"And why is that?" He stopped playing solitary catch and tilted his head toward his friend.

"Are we playing twenty questions? You already know the why."

"Humor me."

Tom quit packing and leaned on the pile. "Because I believe she is in league with a demon, and I need to help her."

"After more than twenty years."

"Yes."

"You're bonkers, you know."

"Maybe I am. But if I don't go, we won't know, will we?" He picked up the stack and slid it into his backpack. He pointed his index finger at Paul. "Toiletries."

"Don't think you can hide in the bathroom and avoid my

questions." Paul threw the paper ball against the desk, and it fell beside the garbage can. He tore another sheet from the spiral notebook on the bed and squashed it into a ball.

"Getting my toothpaste. Settle down."

"One week till graduation and you're flying across the country in search of demons."

Tom stuck his head out of the bathroom, dropping his toothpaste and toothbrush into a Ziploc bag. "One demon. One foster sister."

"Thanks for the correction."

"I'll be back Saturday. Long before graduation."

Paul shook his head, tossed the ball into the air. "I don't get it, Rev. Why now?"

"The Magic 8 Ball said the timing was right."

Paul glanced at the ball on the corner of Tom's desk. They consulted it when they had big decisions to make like if they wanted pizza delivered or picked up. He threw the ball and Tom jumped to the side.

"You missed."

"Asshole."

"I'll only be gone two nights. Boom. I find Olivia, see if she's okay. How the years have treated her. Say hello."

"And exorcise her."

Tom chuckled. "No." He'd be lying if he said he hadn't considered the different scenarios of what could come from this. If she was still involved with Jet. With *Black*. "One step at a time, homey."

Paul checked his watch.

"We've got two hours till Peters' final."

"Yeah, yeah. We both should be cramming right now." Paul ripped out another page.

"I'm too jazzed to study. I'm out right after. 4:30 flight."

"And I'm crammed out." He threw the next ball against the wall. It bounced into the trash. "Three points! And the crowd goes wild!" Dropping onto his back, he bicycled his feet in the air.

There was a knock at the door and Steph poked her head in. "Hey, guys."

Paul sat up. "Stephanie."

"Hey," Tom said. He motioned toward Stephanie. "She knocks."

Paul stuck out his tongue.

"You look great." He gave her a quick kiss and closed the door behind her.

She wore black jeans and a dark grey tee shirt. "Thanks. Nothing fancy."

"Nothing fancy works."

They turned toward Paul.

"Yeah, yeah. I get it," he said. "Three's a crowd." He stood, throwing his last paper ball at Tom and heading for the door. "I'd hate to be a cock block," he said. "Use a condom, kids."

Tom grabbed the balls from the trash and winged them at Paul's back as he ducked out the door.

"What?" Stephanie said. "What was that?"

Tom shook his head. "Don't mind him. His superpower is knowing when to leave."

"See you at Peters', Rev. Bye, woman," Paul yelled from the hall.

Stephanie laughed, but her smile quickly faded. She sat on the bed and pulled Tom's pillow into her lap.

"What's the matter?"

"I went through all the recordings and photos from the other night."

"And?"

"Well," she shifted the pillow, scooching her back against the wall. "We didn't get anything from the Harper house. Absolutely nothing."

"That's good, isn't it? Maybe she moved on?"

Stephanie nodded. "Or it was an off night, and she didn't want to deal with people in her home."

"I hope she crossed over."

"Yeah, me, too."

"What about my old house?"

She shifted again, kicking her shoes off and tucking her feet under the blanket. "That's a little weirder."

His stomach tightened. "Weirder? How?" He sat down on the bed next to her.

"We didn't get anything from your mom. Nothing in photos; nothing in the pics that Carly took outside. No EVPs."

"Okay." He eased up. "So, what's the problem?"

She pulled the voice recorder from her pocket. "We did get an EVP."

"But not my mom."

She shook her head.

"What does it say?"

She hesitated with her finger over the play button, then pressed it. A voice he hadn't heard in decades came through. A voice he barely remembered but struck a chord deep within his mind.

Back off, little boy

He half expected to hear Jet's voice. Black's. And that would have been chilling enough, that low, gravelly voice. But it wasn't.

"Oh, my God," he said.

Stephanie looked into his eyes, which were wide.

"That's Olivia."

Tom stood. His mind was spinning like tires on an icy road. "What does that mean? Is she dead?" Was he too late? Was Wyoming a mistake?

"I don't know. I don't know what it means." She played the track again.

Back off, little boy

"That's her. I'm sure of it." It was definitely her voice. Or Black imitating her, which meant he was on the right track.

"Maybe you don't go to Wyoming?" She didn't want him to go. The EVP was creepy as hell; a freaking whisper directed at him. Commanding him to stop. EVPs were awesome, especially when they connected to investigations or when they got a name, an answer to a question. This, though. This came out of nowhere and targeted Tom. This was all kinds of wrong.

"I have to go. I have to find her."

"Why you? You haven't seen her since you were little."

He took her hands. "It's just something I need to do. My mission. Maybe that's why I was drawn to the ministry . . . because some day she'd need my help. I don't know." He didn't say that he'd always felt insecure. Afraid. And the church quieted that fear. He didn't tell her that he'd never pinned down what had dogged him all these years, what made him need to look over his shoulder, but everything seemed to be coming to head. His memories bubbling up from the sludge he'd hidden them in. This EVP. Something was brewing and he had to confront it.

"Okay. I guess I understand. I only wish you'd stay."

"I'll call you when I'm there and I'll be back Saturday. It'll be so fast you won't even know I'm gone."

"Be safe," Stephanie whispered. "I want you back."

"I'll be back." He hugged her and they stayed like that as long as he dared without missing his flight.

Chapter 23

The stairwell echoed with Reilly's footsteps, and he pushed the fire door at the bottom of the stairs. Thunk. Those doors, no matter how well installed, how new, always thunked. It swung shut behind him and he saw that the door to Olivia's office was propped open, with a man stationed on either side. Not-men. Bloodless faces, blank expressions. His insides sickened.

The energy in the basement was different from the rest of the building. Heavier. More oppressive. Almost as if you walked into a boiler room running full tilt filled with steam. Thick. And those corpses didn't help. He tugged the collar of his shirt away from his neck. Oppressive. That's what it was.

He waited in her doorway while she continued to go through paperwork. The Should-Still-Be-In-The-Grave ghoul named Kyle touched his arm. It made his skin crawl, and he instinctively recoiled, bumping into the one named Garrett.

"Fuck all," he muttered.

Without looking up, Olivia said, "Can I help you?"

"I, uh, was wondering if we could talk?"

She leaned back in her chair and dropped her pen onto the desk. "Personal or business?"

"Business." He felt like a child being sent to the principal's office. Waiting to find out what he'd done wrong. What his punishment would be.

"You don't have to stand there. I've got chairs in here for a reason."

"Thanks. Thank you." Nerves were his specialty lately. Raw,

open nerves. He took a chair across from her, folding his hands in his lap. Unfolding them. Resting them on the arms of the chair.

"You're suspiciously quiet, Brutus. Tongue tied as if thousands of words are fighting to spill out of your mouth. What's up?"

He ran with it. "I don't think I can do this job." There. He said it. His cards were on the table.

Olivia regarded him with a slight tilt of her head. "You've proven yourself to be quite adequate."

His palms were sweating. "That's not what I meant." If she could raise the dead, send spirits to God knows where, what could she do to him?

"You have a free apartment. No rent. Zip. Zero. Zilch."

"Yes. I know."

"And a paycheck, direct deposited."

"Yes, yes. That's not the issue."

"Can't hack the fine print? The little details?" She sat forward. "The dead?"

He averted his eyes. "You know I appreciate all those things, minus the dead part. You've been very generous. But what you did with that Lilith woman," his voice shook. "I don't even know what you did to her."

"You know this isn't the type of job where you can put in two weeks' notice, get a reference and I start interviewing replacements, right? That's not how this works."

"I guess I know that." Reilly swallowed.

"Good.'"

"And that sense of power you crave, doesn't come overnight. That can take years, decades, of hard, dedicated work. You have to prove yourself."

"But I need answers."

"You need."

"Answers."

Olivia smiled, her fingers steepled. "Ask your questions."

Questions whirled through his mind, like dandelion seeds on a breeze. Chasing them, unable to grab any. Grasping at them but not getting them right. Not knowing what to ask. "What did you do to that spirit?"

She closed her eyes, rubbing her temples. "Why do you want to get involved with the minutia? The day-to-day workings?"

"I was there. That already involves me."

She sighed. "I suppose you have a point."

He sat quietly. The ball was in her court.

"Fine. The woman has been there, reliving her death, for many years. I released her."

"No."

"No?" She was enjoying this game, the cat and mouse of it all. He was such fun to fool with, at first fearful, but then finding a little confidence to go with his brutish persona.

"The real reason."

"All right." She stared into his eyes. "Her son was going to show up that night looking for her. I didn't feel it was time for them to connect. She's now my ace in the hole, so to speak, if he comes snooping around here."

"You mean she can come back from where you sent her?"

"Good question." She pondered it. "You know, I don't think anyone has. Or maybe they haven't tried. Either way, I don't think so."

"You don't even know what you did to her?"

"Oh, I know, dear. I just don't know if she can come back from it. She may now be a little jetsam in the ocean of life. Or death, such as it is."

He shook his head. "So, you're using her. Against her son. That's pretty shitty."

"I really don't need to explain myself or any of this to you. Who are you to judge? How do you know her son isn't a piece of shit coming to murder me or something?"

His brow furrowed. He didn't believe her, but it could be true.

People could definitely want to get her out of their lives. "Why the undead? An army against whoever it is coming to get you?"

"Ah, a little snarky, I see. Not an army. They're followers. They're here because I desire undying devotion and service."

"A cult."

"A cult would suggest me bending their will or brainwashing them. Their will *is* my will. They made their deals long before I came into the picture. Vince wanted money and prestige. And don't get me started on Margaret. Kyle and Garrett keep things on the up and up while I work. No surprises rushing in. The others . . ."

"There's more?"

Olivia's eyes sparkled. "There will be."

It was like he'd fallen into a well and couldn't climb out. Move on, next subject, find another way out. "You don't trust me to protect you? You need undead bodyguards?"

"You weren't hired as a bodyguard. And no, I don't trust you one hundred percent. Human beings can be fickle."

"You're human."

"Alas, I am. But I'm special. You might get a wild hair up your ass and head for the hills at the wrong time. Or you might go rogue and think you can leave, and end up like," she winked, "Kyle and Garrett."

He ignored the veiled threat. "Because you're raising the dead and tearing up souls!" He hit her desk with the palm of his hand.

"Temper, temper. Those aren't the only tricks in my arsenal."

He settled into his chair. "The demon gets the souls."

"My *partner* sees his contracts fulfilled." She rolled her eyes. "Not sure what you don't understand."

"And, in return, you get your magic."

"Magic is me pulling a quarter out of your ear and telling you it's from your great grandmother. Power is bringing her back from the dead to give it to you yourself. Whatever you want to call it, I don't care. Black gets what he's owed, and I get to learn from him. It's symbiotic.

A win-win."

He sat in silent disbelief at how he ended up here. Of what he could have possibly done in his life, albeit there were things that were pretty bad, to end up here.

"Would you like Great Grandma to pop in with a quarter for you?"

He mouthed the word no, shifting in his chair.

"This is what you signed up for, Brutus. Your entire life has led you here. To me. To this." She lowered her chin. "Suck it up, buttercup."

He noticed a ripple in the corner of the room. A shift in the energy, like waves of heat rising off pavement in the summer, even though the room was cold.

"Did you know this room used to be the morgue? In the original asylum."

"I, uh. No?"

"That's why I love having my office down here. Absolutely dead quiet. Emphasis on dead. No distractions." She glanced at the corner. "Would you like to meet your employer?"

The temperature in the room dropped twenty degrees as the ripple he'd noticed became a shadow, a seven-foot-tall shape of darkness. A man shaped black hole of buzzing flies. It slid toward him, slick and roaming, pulling itself together and then enveloping him.

Fear stabbed his mind as a putrid odor ripped through his nostrils to his lungs. His stomach heaved. He tried to turn, bend to puke, but was pinned down. Burning bile singed his throat. Glowing eyes bored through his skull, into his brain, while the shadow coalesced a hand that dove deep into his chest. His body seized as the demon gripped his heart, tearing through his mind, sending sewage pumping in his veins.

An avalanche of terror roared through him.

And then it was over.

No promise of power. Only destruction. Control.

Olivia returned to her paperwork as he lay in the chair, shaking. Panting. Finally, he managed to stand, legs weak. Stomach churning. As he stumbled toward the door, Olivia said, "Nice talk. We'll have to do it again sometime. And have your truck ready at 9:00 p.m."

Chapter 24

Tom stood at the Thrifty Rental Car desk with his backpack at his feet. His flight arrived on time and all he had to do was sign the forms for his rental. Sure. All he had to do was sign.

He waited at the desk while the woman in the red Thrifty Rental jacket brought up his reservation on her computer.

"Mr. Anderson," she said, looking over her wire-rimmed glasses. "I see you've gone for our smallest economy car. We've got an upgrade available, ready and waiting on our lot. Full size. A small additional charge, but worth every penny. It's more luxurious and comfort is at the heart of all we do, isn't it? I can make that change for you easily." Her hand moved forward on the keyboard.

"No, thank you. I've fine with the economy car."

"Are you certain? The upgrade has more leg room and I'm sure whoever you're traveling with would appreciate it."

"Thank you, but I'm alone. It's just me and my backpack."

She let out a, "Hm," more a scoff than a pleasant acceptance of his refusal. "We have extra insurance in case of accident or theft. Your insurance may not cover all potential issues that could pop up in the course of your travels."

"I don't think so." The line behind him was growing.

"Well, then, you may very well want to add on our roadside assistance coverage. If you're stranded by the side of the road, day or night, our service people will come out and get you going again."

"I'm sure it's great, but I really don't need it. Not for this trip. Just driving to my destination and returning to the airport to fly home."

"Accidents are called accidents for a reason. Even if it's

something as small as a tire losing air, our people will assess the problem and get you rolling again."

"No, thank you, ma'am. I'd like to get on the road now." He wondered if she'd be at him so hard if he looked older or had worn his collar.

"At the very least I can offer you our prepaid tank of gas. You're aware that the tank must be full when you drop off the car. If you take the prepaid tank, you can bring the car back without stopping to fill it. We'll take care of that. Can I add that on for you?"

"I'm sure I can top off the tank before I bring it in. Thank you, no."

Without another word, she printed the form and had him sign, pointing with her long red fingernail where to put his signature. Then, she handed the keys and a clipboard to a man in coveralls who walked with Tom to the Corolla he was renting. They examined the perimeter, so Tom had a chance to see that it had no damage, only a slight scratch on the back bumper. The man took pictures and said he'd attach them to his paperwork. Another signature.

Once Tom had the keys, he slid his backpack to the floor of the passenger side and got in. It was a nice little car, grey interior, and had that new car spray smell. Probably gave it a spritz before he got there. He pulled up the GPS on his phone. Western Nebraska Regional Airport, code BFF, was about seventy miles from Hartville and it was already after 10:00 p.m. At least he told the hotel he'd be getting in late.

He picked up US 26 and set the cruise control. Sixty-four miles of highway until he hit route 270 N, minutes from his hotel.

The lights in the lobby were low when he wandered in, with one person at the desk flanked by large potted plants. The Ficus was dusty and the dirt was fake, pulled away from the sides of the plastic container with candy wrappers along its base. A solitary light shone over the counter. He dropped his pack to the floor.

"I've got a reservation. Anderson. Two nights."

The hum of the vending machines in the alcove past the desk was the only sound. Even the road outside was empty.

"I need your driver's license and credit card."

He pulled his wallet out of his pocket and gave her the cards. "Quiet night."

"It is." She focused on running his information and activating his key card. "Here you go. Room 217." She gathered everything into a pile and handed it to him. "Card goes in the door, wait for the green light. Remove the card and you can enter the room."

"Thank you. Do a lot of people mess that up?"

"You'd be surprised at how many come back down because they don't wait for the light."

He thanked her again, said goodnight and scooped up his pack. The door to the stairs was past the elevator. No sense in taking an elevator one floor up.

The second-floor hallway, also with night lighting on, was in muted reds and golds. He stood in front of room 217, tapping his card against his fingers. "Insert, wait, pull out, enter. Pretty simple." It opened on the second try.

It was a basic room: a queen-sized bed, television mounted above the dresser. Bolted in place, as if anyone would try to run off with that behemoth on their backs. It was a relic out of the 1950s. A lone hardbacked chair was against the wall. He didn't need much. A place to sleep between meeting Olivia's grandmother and maybe finding Olivia. Quick, to the point. Get answers, fly home. Best case scenario: all is well, no demon in sight. The worst-case scenario was unthinkable.

Tom washed his face and climbed between the stiff hotel sheets hoping he could sleep.

The dream came on fast, sucking him down through the sheets and mattress, depositing him with a thud into the driver's seat of a car. He was on a highway, accelerating into the night.

Sixty-five miles per hour.

Seventy-five.

Eighty.

He hit the button for his wipers as raindrops fell on the windshield, growing larger and faster, blurring the headlights of the oncoming cars and smearing with each swipe of the blades. There were signs on either side of the road. Construction Ahead. Merge Left in ½ mile.

Orange cones littered the road. Barrels. The rain distorted their shapes. The distance.

He glanced at his side mirror, then zipped into the left lane, a horn blaring at him. "Yeah, yeah," he muttered. "Whatever." He gripped the wheel, pressing the accelerator a little harder. Safety versus getting there in one piece. Hard choice.

He was on a mission. A moral imperative.

He clipped a cone to avoid the cement barrier on his left. Nothing would stop him.

A mile to go to exit 113. His turn. It came up quickly, and he braked enough to take it on four wheels, a feat at fifty-three miles an hour. He managed to stop a little past the stop sign at the end of the ramp.

His heart pounded, a metronome set too high.

He accelerated up a hill that was nearly obscured by tree branches and bushes. Debris from the storm was strewn across the road and he had to ease the car around a small tree that had fallen. A bend in the road and ahead of him was a castle.

The castle.

A fortress.

It came into focus as he drove forward. It was large. Abandoned. And the heart of where he needed to be. He parked and climbed out of the car.

Lightning lit the sky as thunder rolled, and he saw what must have been a thousand crows along the castle's stonework. Above windows, entryways. On the walkway. Stoic and still. But he knew they were alive. Of one heart. One mind.

He'd have to get past the birds to get inside. And then he saw the menacing shadow above them, its eyes glowing red, arms outstretched.

And he recognized it.

You are not wanted here

The birds took flight, targeting him. Flying as one massive killing machine. Wind rushed him from the flapping of their wings. The roar of their caws shook the earth under his feet.

He ran. For his life, for his soul, he ran.

Tom woke, legs twisted in blankets, pillows knocked to the floor. Panicked. Hunted. He rolled over groping for the switch to the table lamp, spilling the water glass as he scrambled for light. Praying for protection and peace of mind, he was wide awake until dawn broke. Only then did he feel safe enough to sleep.

A steaming coffee in his cupholder and a croissant wrapped in wax paper in his lap, Tom drove. The sun was bright, and he regretted not putting sunglasses in his pack. He unclipped the visor and swung it to his side window. A great morning for a road trip, even if it was only twelve miles.

He replayed the nightmare from the night before. It could be chalked up to stress, the trip, the repressed memories floating to the surface of the pool in his mind. Or, more accurately, they were like a diver surfacing too fast. His brain had the bends, and he was getting slapped with decompression sickness in his dreams.

"Has to be stress," he said to the empty car. "Finals, graduation, the memories." A truck ahead of him threw on its hazards. Checking his blind spot, he changed lanes and sped up to pass. "Getting this close to seeing Olivia. Touching the past."

He maneuvered into the slow lane, popped open the lid of his coffee and took a mouthful. It was hot, sweet and satisfying. His stomach growled and he remembered his breakfast. Peeling back the paper as he held the wheel one-handed, he took a bite. Greasy flakiness greeted his tongue. Not what he would have preferred, but the continental breakfast was free, and free was free.

He followed the blue road on his GPS screen, and it soon said that in one mile he'd be taking a right onto Burton Lake Road. 1200 feet until the left turn on Magnolia Drive. From there, he was two minutes from Hazel Road and his destination. A low-grade tension grew in him, as if butterflies were having a sword fight in his stomach.

"Just meeting Grandma and having a chat. What's wrong with me?" He pulled into the driveway of a single wide trailer. Yellow daffodils were starting to bloom on either side of the walk. "Here we go."

The homes were spread apart, with plenty of lawn to be mowed between them. He wondered if one of the neighbors took care of Mrs. Hendricks' grass. The house was pale blue, the siding dark under the windows. Nothing a good power wash couldn't cure. He stood on the welcome mat for a full minute before knocking.

An elderly woman in a grey V-neck sweatshirt and sweatpants opened the door. "I wondered if you were going to get around to it."

"Excuse me?"

"You stood there long enough. I didn't know if you were going to knock or not." She smiled, a rosiness growing in her weathered cheeks. "What can I do you for?"

"My name is Thomas Anderson and-"

"Are you selling something? There's not a lot an old woman like myself has need of."

He shook his head. "No. I'm an old . . . friend of Olivia's. I was trying to get back in touch with her."

"Ah, is that it? Come on in, Thomas Anderson. Come on in." She pushed open the screen door. "Have you had breakfast? I've got coffee on but could whip you up something."

"Oh, I've eaten. But thank you for the offer."

"Of course. If you change your mind, speak up." He followed her into the kitchen where she took a mug off a hook on the wall and poured it full. "I like it black. Always have. Drink it all day long, I do. Whenever I get thirsty, I grab a cup and pour another." She sat at the kitchen table. "Have a seat, Thomas."

He pulled out a chair with metal legs and sat. The tabletop felt like linoleum and had a pattern of little blue flowers. Something you could wipe with a damp cloth and call it a day. Easy to clean, looking like something out of a 1950s truck stop.

"You can call me Tom."

"Tom. And you can call me Bernie, but most stick to Mrs. Hendricks. An age-thing, I'd say." She took a sip, closing her eyes and savoring the deep flavor. "So, Olivia, you say. Did you go to school with her? Are you from around here? I don't remember you, I'm sorry."

"No, no. I'm from back East. I knew her when she lived with the Resnicks. I was a foster child for a little while when she lived there."

She clucked her tongue. "Such a tragedy, that. So sad."

"Yes."

"I wasn't ready to be a mom again when she came to me. But family is family, and I made do. It was her decision to live here. They offered her another home back East, but I think she had to get away. It was too hard to stay there." The woman shuddered.

Movement at the window over the sink caught Bernie's

155

attention. She made sure her coffee was safe at the center of the table and got up. She tapped on the window, tap tap tap, then wagged her index finger. "Now don't you be listening in. It's none of your business." A final, tap, and she returned to the table. "When there's a conversation about Olivia, he always shows up. Nosey thing."

Tom bent to see outside, but the bird had gone.

"She has a way with them, you know. The crows."

Crows. Another memory bubbling up from something oil-like, deep within him. Crows. Olivia did have a way with them. *Come here, I'll show you something special.* She introduced him to the crow she was feeding, making friends with. But another came. A larger crow with a darker heart and intention. His butterflies had been right to be stirred up.

And then there was the dream from the night before.

"So, where is Olivia? Is she local? I'd love to see-"

"Oh, no." She took another swig from her mug. "I'm sorry to say that if you came this way just for her, you'll be vastly disappointed. She's back East."

His stomach fell.

"Back East?"

Bernie kept her hands wrapped around the mug, soaking the last bits of heat into her arthritic hands. "Yes. She stayed on here for a while doing various jobs. Saving money." Another sip. "She'd be working two or three jobs at a time, that girl. Cashier at the garden center, bank teller. Even caretaker at a cemetery. Not that I thought that was a job for a girl, but I guess nowadays they can do anything." She bent toward Tom as if telling a secret. "Not that they can, in my opinion. Some jobs are meant for men and their muscles."

"You may be right."

"Where do you work, if I might ask?"

"I'm graduating next week from seminary. Going to be a minister."

"Well, now. That's very nice. You won't get rich doing it, but

156

life isn't about money."

"Very true."

"Did you know Olivia even took up tattooing?"

"I didn't."

"Anything, that girl. If she could try something new and earn some money at it, she'd do it. Constantly in motion, rarely home. But she had a goal and worked hard toward it."

"What goal was that?"

"To get back East. There was a piece of property she wanted to buy. Some apartment building or doctor's offices . . . something like that. Near where she grew up. A place called Freemont or Forestville. She'd tell me, 'That's where the crows are.' Not that we don't have them here, obviously," she said with a nod toward the window, "but she felt back East was the place to be with them. Maybe set up a bird sanctuary. I don't know."

Bernie continued on, about birds, the weather. Flowers in her garden and how she'd be planting tomatoes and onions soon. Green peppers always did well, too. But cucumbers took over, sending their runners all over the place. They gave her indigestion so maybe she'd not plant any.

All Tom could think of was the crows. Olivia wanting to be with the crows and how they barred his way in his dream. Then attacked.

"Do you garden, Tom?"

"I haven't had much chance. Sometime I'd like to."

"Fine, fine. I hope you do. It's very calming."

He pushed away from the table and stood. "I've taken enough of your time, Mrs. Hendricks."

"You can call me Bernie, Reverend Anderson." She got up and hugged him. "Enjoy the rest of your stay here and have a safe trip back."

"Thank you."

They walked together to the door.

"It was very nice talking with you today, Bernie." Tom swung open the screen door.

"It was a very nice chat. I don't get visitors often, but between you and that other gentleman who asked about Olivia, I've had a nice week."

Tom stopped. Turned. "Someone else was here? Asking about Olivia?"

"Oh, yes." She adjusted her glasses. "An older man. He asked a lot of questions. I almost couldn't get a word in edgewise. Said he was from Hilldale, I think, originally."

"Another friend?"

"Must've been, but older. An old teacher of hers maybe. He said he taught."

Tom met her eyes. "By any chance do you remember his name?"

She beamed. "As I remember my own. It was Dominic Russell."

He felt as if his heart stopped.

"Have a nice day, Reverend."

"You, too, Bernie."

She closed the door as his thoughts took flight like the birds.

Russell.

Tom slammed the car door and started the car. The rental came to life, and he slowly backed out of the driveway.

Dominic Russell.

Here asking questions, just like he was. Looking for Olivia. And he had investigated The Forest View apartments in Freemont. That had to be the property Olivia wanted.

The question was *why*.

Now he was a man on a mission, like he had been in the

nightmare. Not only did he have to find Olivia, he had to find them both.

And there would be crows.

Chapter 25

Stephanie saw that the side door to Tom's dorm had been propped open with a rock, and she took the opportunity. It was quicker than heading to the main lobby, past the desk, only to wait in line at the elevators. And she didn't mind the exercise.

She took the stairs by twos and went up three flights. At least it didn't smell like stale beer. The boys' dorms at NCC were a stench of old beer, dirty laundry and sweat. Not pleasant. She arrived at Tom's floor, shoved open the fire door and walked to his room. The hallway was quiet. The guys were either studying or packing. She nodded as she passed one of Tom's friends taking the memo board off the wall. He waved.

She knocked on Tom's door. He wasn't back from Wyoming, but she knew who'd be there.

"Yo!"

She walked in, dropping her purse beside her boyfriend's desk. "Paul."

"Steph." He was lying on Tom's bed, a copy of The Raptor and the Wren by Chuck Wendig in his hands.

"Good book?"

He leaned on his elbow, index finger keeping his place. "The man speaks to me."

Stephanie pulled a notepad and pen from her purse and sat at the desk, opening Tom's laptop.

"Mind if I?"

"Not at all."

She paused, looking at Paul sprawled across the bed. His shoes were untied, and his sweatshirt was rolled into a ball at his head. Tom's pillow was against the wall. A takeout container of what looked like Chinese food sat on the nightstand with a bottle of water on the floor.

"You don't live here, you know."

"Neither do you."

She shrugged, taking an apple out of her bag, and clicked on the Chrome icon. He went back to his reading.

Stephanie searched based on keywords Tom had given her, starting with Dominic Russell. He'd already hit the key articles; they were highlighted in purple. Systematically, she went through Forest View Apartments, New Castle Asylum. Parker Davies. Jack Barnes. Amanda Harper.

She jumped when her phone rang.

"Hey, Steph. What's doing?"

"Tom," she said. "You didn't tell me Olivia had an older brother who was killed."

"Foster brother. And yeah."

Paul stirred in his sleep and his book flipped shut, losing his place. He rolled to face the wall.

"Could you have had anymore trauma in your childhood? Also, how everything seems to tie in is insane. It's layer upon layer upon layer. How's Wyoming?"

"Olivia's not here."

"What? Where is she?"

"Her grandmother says, get this, back there. Freemont."

She planted her feet on the floor. "You're kidding."

"Wish I was."

"At least it only cost the plane ticket," she said. "And now you can meet up with her, I'm sure."

"That's the plan."

She tucked the phone closer to her chin and turned the chair away from Paul. "I miss you. Wish you were coming back tonight."

"Miss you, too. And I'll be home tomorrow."

"See you then."

"Bye."

A muffled, "Miss you, too," came from Paul, his face in the pillows.

"Go back to sleep, you." Stephanie clicked the button to disconnect the call, then dialed Carly. "Hey. What are you doing tonight? I've got a crazy spot to investigate. Murder site. And it happened outside. We can probably get pretty close."

"Get out. Where?"

"Aliton. I'll tell you more when you pick me up."

Carly and Stephanie parked in the Movies! Movies! Movies! parking lot, under the sign that read Parking for Patrons ONLY. The lot was three quarters full.

"We should blend in for the next showing."

"They never check those things unless there's an issue and the 11:00 p.m. movies rarely sell out. We'll be fine," Stephanie said.

They exited the car, both in black leggings and sweatshirts, Carly sporting a black knit cap.

"We look like cat burglars." Carly stifled a laugh and pulled on black gloves.

"Just need ears and a tail." Stephanie checked the batteries in her recorder, then stuffed it into her pocket.

Carly locked the car.

"No camera tonight?"

"I don't know if someone lives in the house or not and I didn't want to call attention to ourselves. This is a sneaky hush-hush mini investigation."

Carly gave a slow nod as she put the keys in her pocket. "Sneaky hush-hush."

"Yup."

"Does Tom know we're doing this?"

They walked down the street, checking house numbers. Names on mailboxes.

"Steph."

"He doesn't know, but I think he'd be okay with it."

"If you're sure."

"I'm sure." She wasn't but thought he should be okay with it. He was deep into discovering all the details of the murders, the so-called demon, figuring out the whys and wherefores. Getting answers. Maybe this would give him something more. "Besides, we'll be outside. You can't get in trouble outside, right? Let's cut across the next lot so we can backtrack behind the houses."

They found themselves among some bushes, next to a chain-link fence. Stephanie crouched as she moved along it.

"I think the yard we want is next. Where the fence ends."

"God, please let me not get arrested tonight," Carly whispered.

"Where's your sense of adventure?"

"It's back in the car."

Stephanie stopped at the edge of the fence. "Looks like your typical backyard."

They sat in the grass, blending in as much as they could with a hydrangea bush. "And how should a murder backyard look?"

As they settled in, footsteps came from the opposite direction and two figures emerged from the shadows: a woman in jeans and denim jacket and a larger male carrying something. Stephanie scooched herself closer to Carly. The figures moved to the center of the yard, seemingly unconcerned about being noticed.

"What are they doing?" Carly whispered.

Stephanie planted her index finger against her lips and clicked the voice recorder on.

#   #   #

Olivia strode to the spot in the lawn where, twenty-two years earlier, her brother had died. Foster brother. Seth. The one she'd nicknamed Sylas. But that was in another lifetime. She held no remorse for his death. No guilt. He'd wanted to "save" her from Black, but when he went for the Ouija board, she had to step in. She *and* Black. The container of gas and the lighter were right there. The guy should have left everything alone. Gone about his life. She stopped his heart rather than watch him burn to death. He had been her "brother," after all.

She put up a barrier between the house and herself. And Reilly. A wall of darkness so they wouldn't been seen. Accomplish what they came for without any distractions.

She felt a spirit nearby, moving as she moved. Watching at the fence line.

"Seth, I know you're here."

Carly looked at Stephanie. She mouthed, "Seth? The one we came to find?"

Stephanie nodded and slid the recorder as far in front of them as she could without being seen. They huddled together, spellbound, not believing what they stumbled onto.

The woman spoke again. "Come on, dear brother. You don't need to be afraid."

A change in energy, a ripple. It moved around the perimeter of the fence, keeping its distance.

"I have a proposition for you."

A pale form shifted closer to the house.

"Remember Blake? You were so tortured by his death. It set so many unfortunate things into motion and you lost control of it all. His life was stolen and yours was ultimately destroyed."

Stephanie squeezed Carly's hand. "Blake?" It was a name she hadn't found in her searches.

They were shoulder to shoulder, pressed together. The red light on the voice recorder glowed in the night.

"You can help him, Sy." Olivia smirked, using the old nickname she'd had for him. It was more from knowledge than memory. Something to be used. Exploited. A means to an end. "You can save his soul."

Olivia motioned to Reilly, and he held out a flat, rectangular board.

"A Ouija board? What the hell is going on, Steph? What are they doing?"

Another squeeze of her friend's hand. "I don't know."

"I don't like this. I don't like it at all."

Fear gripped them both. This wasn't visiting a site and trying for an EVP. This was evolving into something very wrong.

"I've spent these years researching, Sy. Wanting to turn

everything around. Make things right again. If we open the portal and you take my hand, you can pull him out again. You can save his soul and both of you can move on."

Reilly rested a planchet on top of the board.

"Trust me, Sy. This is the only way to get to Blake. And you're the one to do it, since you were with him that night in the mausoleum. You watched while his soul was ripped from his body. You ran away. Fix this, Sy. You were a coward that night, but you can be strong now. Make yourself whole again. Take my hand."

Stephanie watched, jaw dropped, as the pale figure floated closer to the woman. She wanted to yell for him to get away, not to trust what was going on. Her gut instinct was to cry out, yell to him. Warn him. But fear kept her silent.

"Come on, Sy. You know you can trust me. Remember how you'd call me Olive? Can't you see, it's me? Olivia."

Stephanie's heart beat harder. Shock settled into her mind, a tightness in her stomach. Olivia. Tom's Olivia. She was watching the person he'd been searching for. Carly glanced at her, disbelief on her face.

Olivia reached out her arm to the form, which was now only a few feet away. Her other hand rested on the board. She quickly began sliding the planchet around, not looking at what she was doing, but moving with intent. It came to rest, and she kept her hand in position.

"Take my hand, Sy. We can fix this together."

The form solidified and the face of a young man became visible. Sad. Pained. His brow knit together. An aura of unrest surrounded him. Indecision. Longing.

"Please, Sy."

Olive

She knew she had him. She'd broken through his defenses. Grabbed the nerves that were frayed and aching all these years later.

"Yes, Sy. Take my hand."

He reached forward and as he did, Olivia pushed the planchet to its final spot on the board. Hello. She grasped his hand as a swirling, vile vortex rose. Tentacles of darkness wrapped around the spirit, tearing at him as it dragged his struggling form into the portal that had formed. A scream tore through the night as he was torn into the next realm. The vortex fell silent. Closed. Gone.

The air was stiff with emptiness. Muted. As if the air held the quiet vibration. Absence. That edge of sound. Breath held.

"Let's go, Brutus."

"Reilly." He hung his head, tucking the board under one arm.

They left the way they had come, with the man a few feet behind the woman. At the end of the yard, Olivia glanced over her shoulder, "I hope you enjoyed the show, girls. You can tell my little brother I said hello."

With that they were gone, and Stephanie and Carly sat shaking in the bushes.

Chapter 26

The plane taxied in ten minutes early. 2:00 p.m. He had plenty of time to get back to the dorm and relax for a bit before heading with everyone to the Wet Raven or grabbing some dinner with Stephanie. Tom waited for a pregnant woman to exit in front of him, then reached to remove his backpack from the overhead compartment. An elderly man flirted with the stewardess, giving her a wink and a cluck of his tongue, then continued on his way off the plane. Tom smiled and shook his head.

His phone was buzzing in his pocket as he walked to the overnight lot to get his car.

"Hey, Steph. Just landed. What's up?"

"We need to talk."

He stopped walking, phone to his ear, his eyes scanning the area for his car. "What's wrong?" Her voice held a tension he hadn't heard before.

"Hear me out and don't be upset . . ."

"You make me nervous with 'don't be upset,' but okay." He spied his car behind a couple of SUVs.

"After looking through articles about everything, the people from your past, Carly and I decided to do a little investigation outside your old foster house. Olivia's house."

Tom waited, unsure of why she would think that was an issue. "Okay, did you find anything?"

Dead air for a moment, an awkward silence on Stephanie's end. "Steph?"

"We weren't alone, Tom. We got there and two people went

into the backyard ahead of us. It was Olivia, Tom. Olivia and some guy."

He was silent, his jaw working as he tried to comprehend. "How do you know?" But before she could answer, he continued. "What happened? Did she see you? What was she doing there at all?"

"I don't know. It was so weird. She was doing something with a Ouija board and calling out to Seth. Telling him to trust her. That he could help some guy named Blake."

Blake. He knew the name from the articles he'd read. Seth's friend. Seth's dead friend.

"There was a horrible scream, and he was gone. Like he'd been ripped away from wherever he'd been."

"Damn."

"But that's not the end of it."

"I'm afraid to ask."

"I had the recorder running the entire time."

"And?"

"All it got was static. Complete static. It didn't catch what they were saying or Seth screaming or anything. Until the end."

"And?"

She pulled the recorder out of her pocket and turned it on. Holding it close to the phone, she pressed play.

I hope you enjoyed the show, girls. You can tell my little brother I said hello.

She turned it off.

"That's her." Something dark and wretched dropped like a cloak around his shoulders, dragging his mood into the dirt. He clicked the trunk release, but his pack remained by his feet.

"She spoke to us. Knew we were watching her and who we were. How did she know that, Tom? What did she do to Seth?"

He was weighing the questions but had no answers. It spoke

to his concern for Olivia, though. Showed that she'd taken some of Black's power, learned from him. He had wondered if she was in the demon's clutches. Maybe there was hope to get her back on the right path. Maybe she wasn't fully gone.

But *what* did she do to Seth? And why?

"Tom?"

He needed answers more than ever. Her soul was in danger, and he had to find a way to save it. Her. This was why he'd gone to the ministry. This was his reason for being.

"Tom? Are you there?"

"Yeah, Steph." He rubbed the back of his neck, then massaged his eyes with his palm. "I'm here."

"What do we do about this?"

"We do nothing," he said. "I'm going to find Olivia."

Tom typed 'Forest View Apartments, Freemont' into his phone. "Google Maps, don't fail me now." Not that it ever did. His directional sense was crap, and he'd relied on some sort of GPS since day one of getting his license. Good thing finding your way out of a paper bag wasn't on the test, or he'd still be sitting at the DMV.

Fifty-seven minutes. As the crow flies. "Hm," he huffed, putting the car into gear. "As the crow flies." His mind jumped to the vision of black birds covering the outside of the mansion in his nightmare and he wondered if there would be crows at Forest View. He laughed an unconvincing laugh and steered onto Airline Drive, heading toward the highway.

It was a mild spring afternoon, and he cracked open the window. A cool breeze filled the car. As his route took him through Montgomery, he noticed the daffodils had bloomed. House after house had rows of them, yellow and white. It reminded him of Easter and new beginnings. He hoped seeing Olivia would be just that. And if it wasn't, if she was fully possessed . . . he started reading billboards.

Personal Injury? Call our team!

420 Station – Cannabis Dispensary – We're here for U!

Freemont Diner – Best Coffee in the County!

Randy's Liquor Store – Discount Wines and Spirits!

Thanks for the offer, Randy. Hopefully, he wouldn't need it. Reading the signs reminded him of the ones his grandfather would talk about. Burma Shave. They'd have a couple of words on each sign and drivers would have fun piecing them together to get the full message. These weren't catchy or thought provoking and his mind drifted. Returned to worst case scenarios. Olivia could be mentally ill. All this demon stuff, maybe something pushed her over the edge. Hah, something. Like Seth's death. Being nearly murdered. Maybe she was delusional. Thinking she was talking to Seth, luring him. Except she'd known the girls and their relationship to him.

Maybe she'd broken away from Black yet retained some powers. He knew he was grasping at straws. Weak paper straws on a wet table. You don't play with a demon and walk away enriched.

Scenario, scenario.

She could be possessed. Consumed by that thing. He didn't want to let his brain go there, especially since his mission in saving souls and spreading God's word never included any instruction on the realm of demons or their ilk. Sure, the Bible mentioned their existence but only the Catholic church seemed to recognize their presence in the world and tried to do anything about it. He could be facing something he wasn't ready for.

Tom picked up the highway on the other side of town. Twenty-three minutes and he would be within a few turns of the apartments.

His anxiety was palpable. He drove on. No music. No distractions. A single focus. Get to Olivia. He ran and reran conversations in his mind: what he would say, how she would react. If she would recognize him after all these years.

But that was stupid. Of course, she would.

You can tell my little brother I said hello.

Highway markers counted down as the GPS reminded him to exit right in two miles. Goosebumps prickled along his arms. Not only did the voice give him chills, what she said was a punch to the gut. She knew he was looking for her. He had to assume she knew he was coming. It was time to ratchet up his game. Figure out exactly what he was dealing with.

But he knew, didn't he? Knew as much as he let himself. At the back of his mind, brewing, fighting to surface, he knew. Black. Jetty. Olivia had twenty years of working with that thing. Involved with, learning from. He'd assess the situation. Maybe he could talk sense into her. Doubtful, but there was always hope.

Freemont, next exit.

He recited the 23rd Psalm. It was the only thing he could think of as he got closer. "The Lord is my shepherd; I shall not want." He took the exit. Right turn. "He maketh me to lie down in green pastures." Two miles, another right. Over and over, as the road rolled under his wheels. "Yea, though I walk through the valley of the shadow of death, I will fear no," he turned onto the drive to the apartments, "evil." His voice dropped as he pulled into the lot. "Lord, help me."

The building was three stories of red brick. Double entry doors at the front with Forest View above them in large white script. The sign was weathered, as if a remnant of a past era. He could be looking at any apartment building on any street in Any Town, USA, and yet it wasn't. There was a feeling about the place that he couldn't put into words. Couldn't put his finger on. As if it had a pulse. A living, breathing thing that had no right to be a part of this world. The entire area felt wrong. As if he were in a dark alley alone, knowing he was watched. Hunted. Doomed. But it was afternoon. Still daylight for a little while on a beautiful day. Tom put the car in park and switched off the engine.

There were no daffodils.

At least it wasn't the castle from his nightmare.

The lot had two vehicles: a Lexus and a pickup. He clicked the fob to lock his car as he walked toward the front of the building, then turned and clicked twice more. It was locked. He knew it was locked. But it didn't feel secure enough. Nothing here felt safe, and he was filled with unease. Nerves on fire. He touched the cross under his shirt.

A man on a mission. One foot in front of the other.

Tom pushed open the front doors, stepping into the lobby of the building and was greeted by a tall man in a black turtleneck shirt.

"I'm sorry. We're not taking tenants yet." The man blocked his way. Arms crossed. He seemed out of place in his dark suit, overdressed for an apartment lobby.

An odor of decay teased Tom's nostrils. "I'm here to see Olivia Mulvey."

Another man, larger and barrel chested, approached from the hallway ahead of him, past suit man.

"She isn't seeing anyone right now."

"Now, *Reilly*, of course I'm available for my little brother."

The voice came from his left. Olivia, not the fifteen-year-old from his memory but a grown woman, appeared from the stairwell. Her hair was in a ponytail. She wore jeans with the knees ripped out and an old sweatshirt. The look of someone working on their home. The stench of decay was replaced by lavender.

"Yes, ma'am." The large man went back to what he'd been doing while the suit guy returned to his station.

"Tommy, how are you?" She took his hand and practically dragged him toward the stairs. "Come down to my office so we can

174

talk."

He jerked his hand away, startled. It was freezing. Like holding ice.

"Oh, sorry. We're renovating, and I haven't gotten all the quirks out of the heating system yet. It's a little chilly."

He followed her down the stairs, a dizziness taking hold as he reached her office. For a moment, the hallway spun. He put a hand to his head and leaned against the doorframe.

"That stairway and these floors." She tapped the cement with the toe of her ankle boot. "Not at all flat. It can get you loopy until you're used to it. One more thing on the list of renovations."

He nodded, getting his bearings.

"My office used to be the morgue, isn't that the coolest?" She ushered him inside.

The room was unnerving. Not because she'd said it had been a morgue, that didn't bother him. It was the vibration of the place. A low oscillation, off key from the rest of the world. Like animals before an earthquake before it hits.

"How are you, Olivia?" He clasped his hands together to hide his trembling.

"I'm fine, and you, Reverend?"

He sat in the chair in front of her desk. "So, you keep tabs on me?"

"Better than you did on me, I'd say." She clucked her tongue. "Flying all the way out west and for what?"

"Well, I found you. That was the point." She was playing a game, and they both knew it. Cat and mouse, tease and deflect. "Your grandmother was very helpful."

"Ah, yes. Old gran." Doddering old woman. Grandma had been a good shield while she learned and perfected her illusions. Even tried them out on her and she never had a clue.

"I got your message. Your hello." He watched like a hawk for her reaction. Any reaction.

"That was clever, wasn't it?" She wore a self-satisfied smile.

"Creepy, if you ask me."

"I didn't ask you, did I? I was letting you know that you should be careful what you seek. Be careful what you ask for, don't they say?"

"Be careful what you work with, I'd say."

"He's not a what, little brother. He's a he."

"He's a lie." A headache was forming over his eyes. A throbbing migraine. It came back to him how Seth's head used to hurt. How he'd take what seemed like handfuls of pills to make it stop.

Olivia shuffled papers.

"And what about Seth?" He hoped to touch her heart. Make her feel. Pull out a little of the girl he knew when he was younger. The one who loved Seth like a brother, like the only person who understood her.

She peered at him over the rim of her glasses. "What about Seth? Don't tell me you believe in ghosts, too? Your girl sure does."

"What did you do to him?"

"Seth died more than twenty years ago. He had no business hanging around that house in this day and age. I simply moved him along. Crossed him over. Before your girl could use him for her own entertainment. She's the one in the wrong here."

"That's not why she was there."

"Then why? To ask him questions, see if he'd talk on that little device of hers. And to what end? For her own shits and giggles. A little excitement. Ooh, I caught a ghost. Ooh, ahh."

"Steph said he screamed before he disappeared."

Olivia shrugged. "Many often don't like the fate they chose."

"Or that chose them."

"You say tomato; I say tow-mah-tow." She considered him for a moment, then changed the subject. "I heard you visited your mother's house."

He stiffened, lips narrowing to a thin line. "I don't want to discuss my mother."

"But you must've gone there for a reason."

"And?"

"She wasn't there, was she?" Another sly smile.

"No. Why?"

Seconds ticked with Olivia wearing a Cheshire Cat smile.

"What are you implying?"

"Nothing, dear. Just giving you things to think about."

"You talk in riddles." He shifted, crossed his legs.

"I don't. A riddle would be: what has hands but can't clap or something about a raven and a writing desk. Or crow. Choose your bird."

"Would you stop playing games? I thought we could have a decent conversation."

"Yes. I'm already tired of it." She sighed. "I thought you'd be a little more fun. Why are you here?"

"I want to help you."

With that, Olivia roared with laughter. Her eyes watered and she had to grab a tissue to dab at them. "Sorry, sorry," she said. "With what?"

His jaw tightened. "You know with what. You're in league with a demon. You of all people should know this can't end well. You, with all your paranormal knowledge. Come on, Olivia."

"Still jealous after all these years that your friend chose me? That's really unbecoming. Or is it your desire to bring a lost sheep into your fold? Start a congregation in Churchy-ville with your long lost but now found sister? Baptize me in a river somewhere and put a notch on your bedpost?"

"What?!"

"Okay, notch on your altar. Not that it would be incest, honey. You were a foster brother."

"You never used to be cruel."

"It's not cruel. It's honest. Bold. In your face. It's recognizing what's inconsequential in this life. If you don't matter, why should I care?"

"You've changed. Black's changed you. There's a darkness in you that didn't exist when we were young."

"Darkness has always existed. Long before we came along. But you've got it wrong. He can give me the world, and I'm happy to take it. You have no idea the things I can do. The power I wield. And I'm still learning."

"And why do you think he's doing that? It's not for you or the good of mankind. It's for his own amusement. It's for your soul."

She leaned back, hands steepled. "You certainly adored him when you were young. Kind of brought him to our house, didn't you? I could credit you for bringing us together in the first place, brother." She emphasized the word, long and low.

"I was too little to understand." His head pounded. Regular, rhythmic. Keeping time with his pulse. "The demon preyed on me and left to latch onto you. But you were too damn hungry for the ghost world to know better. You didn't look before you leaped."

"You had your taste of the darkness, Reverend. If he hadn't left you, where would you be today? Huh? Probably dead or in an alley somewhere with a needle stuck in your arm. You wouldn't be making an empire like I am. Tell the truth." She locked eyes with him. "You can't tell me that being this close to him doesn't tug at you. You can't tell me you don't miss him."

She glanced at the corner, where a shadow had formed into the shape of a cat. A deep, gravely laughter, like boulders down a hillside, formed in his ears. A part of him, the tiniest part, ached for his old friend. Longed for the comfort of his childhood when he had no one else. A familiarity like no other.

He forced himself to look away. "There's good and evil in this world, Olivia. A man has to choose a side." He kept his eyes riveted on the woman before him, trying to ignore the shadow in the corner. The shadow cat crept closer, emanating waves of energy that washed over him like the ocean to the shore. Promising to stop the pain that was pulsing through his head. "I want to save your soul."

Again, laughter from his sister and a booming echo around him.

He gripped the arms of the chair. "I won't let a demon continue to walk this earth and I won't let you be damned!"

Her tone became serious, her voice quiet. "You don't belong here, Reverend. It's time for you to go."

She motioned dismissal with her hand, and something pulled him from the chair. Fear washed over him like an icy shower.

Two of Olivia's followers appeared at her doorway.

"Escort the minister out of the building, boys."

Kyle and Garrett stepped to the side so Tom could pass between them.

"And Rev?" she said. "Three strikes and you're out. Your girl being at my old house was one. This is number two. Don't let there be a third. It won't be pretty."

"I'll pray for you."

"Pray for yourself."

He turned on his heel, brushing Kyle's shoulder. It felt like a spongey press into rotting flesh. He recoiled. A dusty, death-odor rose from the man.

Tom hurried out to his car. The moon had risen, and he heard the beating of wings behind him.

Chapter 27

Olivia was antsy. Since Reverend Tom left, all she'd done was push papers around her desk. A bill on this stack, a bill on that one. Renovation information, invoices for parts, insurance. Shove and shuffle. Nothing getting done. If she were a smoker, she would've lit one up. Maybe two or three. The boy had a lot of balls showing up.

"Ugh!" She slapped a stack of papers and shoved herself away from the desk. "Why didn't you step in? Do something more than cat around?"

What more should I have done

"I don't know. Get rid of him. Something!" She paced.

In due time

"In due time. In due time." She threw her hands in the air.

There is a process
A finesse

"And when are you going to give me more? It's been a while. A long while. Live up to your promises."

Black descended upon her, one tentacle twisting in her hair, pulling her head back. She gasped as he slammed her into the wall with his now-formed body. His voice, gravely and thick, came from all sides.

Your sense of entitlement is disturbing

A sickening smell of sulfur wafted from his mouth, an inch from her own. It burned inside her nostrils, and she didn't want to breathe in, fought depositing that pain into her lungs. His tongue split like a snake's and uncurled. It twisted onto itself, testing her cheeks and lips before it formed into a thick piece of meat, and dove into her mouth, pushing to the back of her throat. A sewage tongue that seared as it probed. Her stomach lurched.

It slid down into her stomach and beyond, infiltrating organs, pouring into her bones. Olivia choked, trying to wrench herself away. The tentacles held her. The body against her, stone. She flexed her own tongue, arching it to remove the bloated animal flesh rotting in her mouth, but it forced itself farther until her lips threatened to split. Hot breath enveloped her face in waves.

"Hey, Olivia, I-" Reilly stepped into the room.

An arm shot toward him. It plowed into his chest, throwing him into the hallway. The door shut and locked.

We work together yet are entirely separate
I can make you see

An evil, black venom flowed through her veins and into her mind. She saw through his eyes. Saw herself beneath him, dwarfed by his immensity. Her vision expanded in waves, and she saw like an eagle. High above Forest View, sense-seeing. She could feel the energies of the people beneath her. Know them.

The power was overwhelming, and she craved it like an addict.

And I can remove that sight

His mind pulled back from hers and blindness took her. The room was utterly devoid of light, an emptiness deeper than space with no stars. There was only sensation and fear. Black's maggot tongue retreated, then plunged deeper, wrapping around her heart. Squeezing her lungs. Terror replaced the contagion in her veins. He could leave her this way. Ruin her. She was small. Vulnerable.

Her vision returned, but the icy air around her remained. The maggot tongue still pulsed venom throughout her mind. Body. Spirit.

Know this
I bestow gifts at my discretion
What is given
Can be taken away

Her body convulsed as her eyes rolled backward. The world clouded.

Do not forget who I am

He withdrew, letting her fall to her knees, then swirled into a roaring mass of flies and disappeared.

She curled into a fetal position and ran a hand through her damp hair. Her stomach was gurgling, nausea roiling. Grabbing the trash can, she vomited until her ribs were sore and her stomach empty. The taste of bile in her mouth replaced the roadkill flavor he'd imparted.

She wiped her face on the back of her hand.

"No lessons today, I take it," she said, glancing around the room.

Olivia stood, holding her stomach, and unlocked the door. Swinging it open, she leaned outward. Reilly was standing under a sconce, looking pale.

"Did you want something?" She held onto the doorframe, more to stay upright than to strike a pose.

"I, uh. You okay?" His legs were weak. Wobbly.

"I'm fine. Don't I look fine to you?"

"What was that?"

She waved him off. "Power comes at a price. Sometimes the boss gets a little testy."

"Testy."

"Yes."

"The boss."

"Right again." She cracked her neck. "If you don't have any other questions, get the board and meet me on the second floor."

Reilly paused before the large door to the storeroom. He preferred to think of it as that, rather than what Olivia dubbed it. The Sanctuary. He shuddered. The Ouija board was kept in the storeroom. Among other things. He tried not to look around, not to take it all in. Not see what looked like an altar or that everything was shrouded in black. Or that there was a ceremonial throne in the corner. Not disturb anything . . . or anyone . . . that might be there.

The thought terrified him, but he was in too deep. He knew he couldn't run before they'd be on him. Olivia. Her *followers*. Bunch of undead security guards was more like it.

Undead. How the fuck did he get himself into this? Sucked in by that kiss. It called to his desires, sent electricity through him. That woman had power, she was right about that. He had been drawn to it like a moth to a flame. And here he was, smack dab in the fire.

Chapter 28

Brian hid in a room on the third floor when he heard them coming. He'd explored all the rooms over the years, in between reliving his death and countless hours of gut-wrenching survivor's guilt. "Surviving-after-death guilt," he mused. The room, 301, was L-shaped and it gave him some small semblance of comfort. Safety. He didn't know why. But it was the highest floor, farthest from the back of the building.

301. As empty as the other rooms. It had a secluded balcony that overlooked the side lawn. Pretty, but he had no use for it. His life was inside. Roaming the halls. Stuck in this place with all the time in the world to scrutinize every inch of every brick. Every inch except the basement. That he avoided like the plague. He kept to the main and upper floors and investigated through the wee hours of the morning, discovering little things: pennies, a pencil, a sticker that must've fallen from a window glass or peeled off a wood sill. Bits of paper. A dead fly. He concentrated on that fly for a week before he discovered how to fine tune his focus and flip that bug over. When it tipped onto its side, he danced and jumped, arms in the air. Celebrating. He could interact with his environment and interaction was key.

From that day onward, his time gained purpose. When he wasn't keeping an eye out for the woman named Olivia and her flunky, he studied. Gathered his strength and attention and switched from object to object, the tiniest ones first. The fly was nothing now. He could whip it around the room, and did, until it began to fall apart. A leg here, piece of wing there. It was time to move on. Bigger. Heavier. The sticker, then the penny. Still working on that. He'd get the edge lifted, a little, and it'd drop.

There were more things to try, though, since the lackey set up shop in 104. He checked that out the day after the guy moved in. What a slob. His blankets were tossed aside, clothes on the chairs and his toothbrush lay across the edge of the bathroom sink. Brian hit the toothbrush as soon as he saw it and watched it spin. A little. Enough that it was caught off balance and fell into the basin. He let out a whoop and holler, but silently to not draw attention. His practice was paying off, his abilities growing stronger.

As the days went by, he'd bring what he could back to his room.

But he had to be careful. For a long time, the demon's presence had lessened. He was forever checking over his shoulder, keeping his distance and avoiding its "area." It was back now, and this woman was dripping with its essence. As if they walked hand in hand, even when the thing wasn't present. They were connected.

And she wanted him. She was after his soul and he knew if she got too close, she'd have it.

He slunk into the shadows of 301's closet and hunkered down.

Chapter 29

Reilly followed Olivia up the stairs to the second floor. "I don't know why we couldn't take the elevator," he grumbled. The smell of freshly painted walls made him queasy.

"Suck it up, Brutus. And be quiet. I'm trying to sense him."

"Him who?"

She stopped mid-step, gripping the railing. Hard. "The ghost who hangs around the second floor. He's like an annoying bug in my house and I want to squash him. Is that all right with you?"

"Okay, okay." He transferred the board to under his other arm. "Was just curious."

She exhaled and continued. Exasperated. It had already been a crap day, and he didn't help her mood. All she wanted to do was trap Brian, grab his stinking soul and have a drink. A nice gin and tonic in her office, shut off from the world.

She trudged on. Frustrated that he was hanging around her place. Their place. Black should have taken his soul when he took Brian's life. Opening the fire door, she waited, Reilly behind her.

"Brian, are you here?" She said it as sweetly as she could muster. He wasn't far. A step. Three. "Brian? I only want to chat with you."

Reilly matched her movements. Quiet. Not wanting her wrath. Wishing for her abilities. He couldn't feel the spirit, couldn't follow it from place to place. As they walked farther down the hallway, one of Olivia's bootlickers appeared from the far elevator. Anders. A short, weaselly man in a cheap blue suit. Reilly thought Olivia should change their clothes, have them wear something more natural. Less funeral-like. Maybe then he could deal better when they crossed paths. Maybe then he could pretend they weren't decaying cadavers.

Maybe he could ask her to mask their odor, too. The stench was building up. With every new corpse, it smelled more like a depository for month old roadkill, tinged with vomit and blood. The death-stink penetrated his nostrils. Saturated his lungs until it was all he could taste. Choked him.

Another came up the staircase and pushed past him, bumping into his shoulder. "Sorry," it said. Putrid breath assailed him.

Reilly cringed, his butthole tightening and his balls threatening to crawl inside him. He hated these fucking things.

Olivia nodded as it walked by. "Mort."

Mort. She'd taken to calling them all Mort. Short for mortuary or mortify. Mortality. Their names didn't matter; they weren't people. They were animated corpses whose embalming was wearing off. Reilly sniffed, quickly regretting it. The dead-rot death smell was increasing. He coughed.

"Shh." She waved her hand at him.

"Sorry. Your army stinks."

She set her jaw and flicked her wrist. A wave of lavender washed over him, replacing the roadkill scent. Another illusion, but one he appreciated. She walked on.

"Brian, we need to talk." But the second floor was quiet. Vacant. She had a sensation that he was higher. Farther. "Brutus. Third floor."

Olivia stalked him with her fingers spread, as if she were trawling for him. "He's up here," she whispered, more to herself than Reilly. "He's close."

They paused at each door. 309. 307. She'd shake her head, and they'd move to the next. 303. A little longer wait. A head shake.

301.

She rested her hand on the wood. Signaled to bring Reilly closer. "Brian, I'd like to speak with you."

No response. She tried the knob, but it wouldn't turn. Taking a ring from her pocket, she found the key and inserted it.

It wouldn't turn.

"Here. Make yourself useful." She stepped aside for Reilly to fix the problem.

Reilly kneeled down. He looked at the keyhole, removing the key and brushing it with his thumb before reinserting it. Steadying the knob with his left hand, he jiggled the key, twisting it to the left and right. There was no metal on metal click. No movement. The lock wouldn't engage.

Olivia scowled and stared at the ceiling, arms crossed. "Come on. Come *on*."

"Nothing. The cylinder's not catching. It's not turning on the inside. Something's blocking it."

She fumed. Furious. "Listen, Brian," she said, her voice raised to an angry pitch. "We're going to get to you if we have to take the entire fucking door off its hinges. I'm done playing around. Your time here is short. I don't want to talk. I mean to send you into the vortex. Got it? Until we meet again, ghost boy."

She pivoted and strode away.

Reilly hung his head and followed.

Brian stayed in the closet until he was sure they were gone. There was only so long he'd be able to hide from her. For now, though, the papers he'd jammed into the lock had saved him for another day. He'd need to come up with a plan.

Olivia marched through her office and went straight into her apartment. She opened the corner cabinet in the kitchen, pulling out a bottle of Bombay Sapphire. One liter. "Too bad they didn't have soda sized." Setting it on the counter, she grabbed a bottle of tonic and a lime from the refrigerator. She pulled the ice cube tray from the freezer, wrenching it to loosen the cubes and dropping three into a glass.

Reilly deposited the Ouija board on her desk. He called out, "What's next on the agenda?"

"A tall stiff one. You want?" She poured the gin.

This was the first time she offered anything more than a condescending, snarky comment. Maybe a drink would relax her attitude. And he was never one to turn down good gin. "Yeah, that'd be great." He walked through her living room and made his way to the kitchen. "Appreciate it."

She took a second glass out of the cupboard. "Don't stand out there, then. Get your ass to the table."

Olivia mixed his drink and sat. It was a small round table, barely fitting into the end of her kitchen. If she wanted to open her storage cabinets, she'd have to bend and practically crawl under it to retrieve anything. Reilly took the other chair. He would have preferred to sit across from her, giving them space, but was instead to her right. Arm's distance. Not exactly comfortable, but alcohol would help.

"Sucky day." Stretching her legs, she crossed her ankles. They brushed against his sneakers. She raised her glass. "Salut."

"Cheers." He clinked his glass against hers and downed half his drink.

"Easy there, Brutus, or you'll be on your second before I finish this."

"Keep up." He ran a finger down the side of the glass, wiping the condensation that was forming. He swiped it across his jeans.

"Oh, I can keep up. You'll be under the table, and I'll get back to paperwork."

"Big words." He raised his drink. "We'll have to see about that." He finished the rest and put the empty glass on the table. No one he'd ever known could call him a lightweight when it came to alcohol.

The corners of her lips curled up, just enough to be noticeable. "Make yourself another."

"Don't mind if I do." Ignoring the lime, he poured half a glass of the Bombay and matched it with the tonic. Then, he turned and added gin to Olivia's glass. "Ma'am."

She sat up straight. "Well, now. I guess we're serious drinking."

"You bet. Best way to take the edge off a shit day."

"I hear that."

He raised his glass and drank it down, then tipped his chair onto its back legs. The backrest knocked into the counter. "Sorry." He half expected a tirade, but she took another sip.

"No worries."

He lowered his chair to the floor. His knee sliding into place beside hers. Resting against hers. "Small space."

"It works for me. I don't spend a lot of time in here. Living room's not bad, bedroom's bigger." Another mouthful. She could feel the heat spread through her face, her cheeks a little warmer than they had been a few minutes ago. The gin was tempering her mood. "Do you want to?" She motioned for them to get up.

"Oh, sure, sure." His buzz was taking hold and if she wanted to head into the bedroom, he could drop his trepidations about being in this end of the building. Forget what a bitch she could be. For a little while, anyway. He moved toward the bedroom as she walked into the living room. Damn it. Wrong again.

"Mistakes were made," she said, as she sat on the sofa and crossed her legs. It was lined with large pillows at either end, turning its sitting space into more of a loveseat.

He grabbed the bottle of Bombay and walked into the living room. "I haven't been in here before. Got lost." A sheepish smile crept

191

over his face.

"Yeah, you're not drunk. Tell me another."

He laughed, looking at his shoes. "More?"

"Sheesh, man. Let me finish this."

He sat, putting the bottle on the floor. Turning to face her, he looked for a spot to set his glass. Behind Olivia was an end table, and he reached across her, his chest brushing against hers. She put a hand on his chest, giving him a little shove. He took his time setting the glass down, positioning it just so and slowly eased himself back to his seat.

"You're a little obvious, no?"

"Blame the gin."

She snorted, taking another sip of her drink. "The gin is fine. I blame the man drinking it."

Reilly shrugged, placing his hand on her knee and letting his fingertips duck beneath the torn denim. Olivia decided to play along, where normally she would have given him hell for it. Let him have fun, think he was the one calling the shots. It didn't take long for his entire hand to be on her thigh under the threads. He squeezed.

Olivia uncrossed her legs, giving him slightly more room, which he eagerly accepted. His hand, although constrained, roamed from side to side, gently rubbing her thigh. She watched him over the top of her glasses. She could tell he was lost in thought, eyes half lidded and not quite focused on her. He was probably on top of her in his mind, a conquering animal. Cat and mouse, Brutus, she thought. We'll see who conquers whom.

"Don't you want this?" She twisted to reach for his glass, raising her ass a bit. Arching her back as she leaned across the arm of the sofa.

"I do." It came as a growl, thick and hungry.

The roughness of his voice excited her. Even if this was a game, she liked the way he was playing. As she sat back, his drink in hand, he slid his right hand up under the back of her shirt, his other hand still on her thigh.

"What should I do with this?"

"Drink it." He ran his hand to her neck and pulled her close. He nuzzled her, kissing along her throat, running his teeth across her skin as he pressed deeper. Pulling his hand from her jeans, he went up under her shirt, under her bra. Tight against her breast.

She closed her eyes, enjoying his calloused hands kneading her soft flesh. Taking the last mouthful from his glass, she let it fall gently to the floor. She could get used to a little attention from time to time, even if it was from Brutus. *Reilly.* In her mind, she rolled her eyes. She scooched forward, pressing into the motions of his hand.

He gripped her breast and leaned against her, taking her down onto the sofa. He used his leg to bring hers under him, then steadied himself with one foot on the floor. He found her mouth.

She turned her face. Kissing was an intimacy he wasn't allowed.

Fuck it, he decided. If that was how she wanted it, fine. He wasn't above getting his nuts off and leaving tenderness out of it. He shoved her shirt up and found her nipples, running his fingers over the hard tips. Another arch of her back, a lick of her lips. A tease till the end.

Reilly ran his tongue across the hard bead, then sucked it into his mouth, all the while keeping his eyes on her face. As she watched him.

One hand still holding her breast, he popped open the waist button of her jeans. The zipper fell halfway on its own. Her panties exposed, he shoved his hand beneath the elastic. Her mound was smooth, shaved, and he gripped it before sliding lower, dancing fingertips across her slit. Tracing its length and back again.

He pulled back. Trace, touch, tease. He'd make her desperate with need. Make her drip for him. Beg. He parted her lips with his finger, slipping between the folds. A light touch of her clit and she shuddered. She spread her legs a little to give his hand more room.

"Good boy."

"I'll show you a man." He couldn't take it any longer. "Come here." There was a gruff urgency in his voice. Running his hands down her back, he grabbed her ass and dragged her toward him, then yanked his pants to his knees. His cock was rock hard, and he pushed her panties to the side, guiding himself to enter her in one thrust. She was tight and wet, and her hips rose to meet him.

His leg slipped, kicking the Bombay bottle. Nothing mattered but how he felt inside her.

With one hand under her ass, he began slowly. Sliding out, plunging in. Rocking. His eyes were shut. Olivia let out little gasps with every thrust.

"Faster," she whispered.

"No." He was in charge for once. He was making the rules, and he was going to enjoy where he was.

She dug her nails into his arms.

He stared into her eyes.

"Faster." He heard it inside his mind this time. The thought was not his own, not his desire. He fought it. He pulled out to just the tip and teased himself, tormenting her. She arched, trying to take all of him.

"Faster."

A command so strong, so compelling. He gave in.

"You want it faster?" The sweat was dripping off his chest. He guided her ankles over his shoulders and grabbed the arm of the sofa, plunging into her. Hard. Fast. No thought of her or of himself. Only feeling. Only his cock as far inside her as he could go, until she exploded against him. He thrusted until the waves of her pussy clutching him finally slowed. He was panting. Sweating.

Shivering. The temperature in the room had dropped by at least fifteen degrees. He lost his erection and grabbed at his pants. Olivia fixed her bra, her jeans. She stood and stretched. A sense of dread, anxiety and darkness filled the air around them. It didn't seem to bother her. To him, it was time to hightail it out of there.

"Hey, uh." He didn't know what to say. How to address what

had happened between them.

"This," she motioned back and forth between them, "is not a thing."

"Right."

"It's not a friends with benefits thing. It's not a 'fuck the boss on Friday' thing."

"It's Saturday."

She rolled her eyes, zipping her pants. She adjusted her shirt. "Whatever. This means-"

"Nothing. I know."

"Good. As long as we're on the same page."

His shoulders slumped a little. Not that he was looking for anything more. Or a fuck the boss thing. He was, in fact, vaguely terrified of her, but he wasn't prepared for wham, bam, thank you, Brutus. She was colder than the room had become. Evil on ice.

"You didn't need to get into my head."

"You should have listened."

"In some things people let themselves go. You don't always have to be in charge."

She chuckled. "I am always in charge." Olivia walked to her office and started pawing through the papers at her desk. She called to him. "You've got some time before we need to head out tonight. Be ready by 9 p.m."

He zipped his pants. "Okay."

As he walked out the door, she said, "I'll give you this, Brutus. You're better than a dildo."

He cringed and his cheeks flushed as he entered the hallway. Not that it mattered if the Morts heard. It was still embarrassing. Emasculating. It didn't take much more than a warm body to beat a dildo. But he did know he'd never touch her again. He'd been used. Used for sex, used to raise the dead and tear up souls. He'd been taken to hell and didn't know if he could ever escape.

Reilly went to 104 and took a hot shower to scrub her off his skin.

But even in the shower, his thoughts drifted to her body against his. In that moment, he hated himself.

Chapter 30

Dom stepped out of Matt's Convenience Store, bag in one hand, cane in the other. Hooking the cane over his arm, he searched the bag for the sunglasses he bought. Ripping the tag off, he put them on. The car that had been in the lot at his P.O.'s office was a few spots down. Two people inside. His instincts told him they were following him. Reporters? Not after this long. Thrill seekers? Intrusive pains in the ass who wanted to get a look at a potential murderer? He grasped his cane and began the two-block walk to the halfway house.

A car door slammed behind him.

"Mr. Russell?"

It was a girl's voice. He didn't break stride.

"Mr. Dominic Russell?"

"I don't give autographs."

The girl caught up quickly.

He stopped walking and looked at the sky. "I don't give interviews. I don't give TED talks. I'm not available for your PTA or whatever the hell organization you're with. I won't join your witch's circle or help you summon demons. And if you're into dating convicted felons, I'm too old for you."

"Whoa."

"Exactly."

"It's not like that at all."

He sighed. "You know my name, and I don't know yours. You and your friend," he leaned forward, looking at the cars parked along the street, "followed me from the parole office. You know my whereabouts. Don't you think that's a little disturbing?"

"Well, when you put it that way, yeah. But."

"There you go. If you follow me further, I'll call the police. You and your friend," he waved at the car, "have a nice day." Dom resumed walking.

"We need to talk to you."

He ignored her, making his way to the stop light at the crossroad. He pushed the button to wait for the white walk-light.

"It's about Olivia."

His back stiffened, frustration growing.

She jogged to where he was standing. "My name is Stephanie. Tom's in the car."

His eyes narrowed. "Look," his voice was tense, "if you've got something to say, say it. But it's none of your business what happened two decades ago."

She shook her head. "Not two decades ago. Now. The guy in the car, that's Tom Anderson. He was Olivia's foster brother when everything happened."

"Damn it." He took a step backward, palms up. "You could cost me my parole. I can't be anywhere near him. Do you understand that?"

"Yes. That's why I came up to speak to you. Let me give you his phone number."

"No." He rubbed his temples. "I can't have his number in my phone. This could ruin everything."

"He has to talk to you. He needs answers. Things are going on. Bad things."

"Of course they are."

"Please, Mr. Russell."

Thoughts upon thoughts. They seemed to be on the level. Seemed. However, this kid could blow up his parole. Send him back to prison. On the other hand, maybe he knew something that would help destroy the demon once and for all. Maybe.

"Call my P.O. God, he's going to kill me for this." His mind cycled through all the iterations of what could come from this, and none of them were good. Worst case scenarios with a thread of possibility. "His name is Bob Walters. Tell him I said to arrange a meeting. I don't care where or when, just discreet. More than discreet. He'll call me, I'm sure. Probably raise holy hell. But he'll do it. I'm sure."

"Thank you. We'll do that. Thank you, Mr. Russell."

"What the hell are you thinking?!"

Dom held the phone away from his ear. He'd known the kind of beating he was going to take. "I have to do this."

"You damn well do not. I put my career on the line with that last stunt."

"It wasn't a stunt, and you know it."

"Yeah, yeah." Bob went silent.

"I need to hear what this kid has to say. He was there the night that Seth died. That Olivia bailed. He may know something I can use."

"Use? What do you mean, use?"

"He may know something." Dom wandered around his room as they talked. He stopped to look out the window, peeking between the blind slats. Robins were scattered across the lawn. A lone crow landed on a branch across the yard. Dom didn't take his eyes off the bird. "He may just want to talk, hear my side of it all. I don't know. But it sounded urgent."

"Maybe he wants to get you put away, too, did you ever think of that? Get seen with you and have your ass hauled back to prison before you can sneeze."

"I don't think so. It would have been easy to do that. Just come up on me and start something."

"So, he's more devious. I don't like it, Dom."

"We could meet in your office."

"The fuck you will."

"Makes sense. Private. You could even stay, make sure things were on the up and up, if you wanted. Know what's going on from the get-go."

"And lose my damn job."

"This is bigger than your job."

"Fuck you."

"So, you'll do it?"

A slight hesitation. "Yeah, I'll set it up." He sighed. "We'll both land in jail."

"Roomies." Dom grinned. "Thanks, man. You're the best."

"That's what they tell me."

Dom plugged the phone in to charge and glanced out the window. The crow was gone. He closed the blinds and wiped the dust residue onto his pants. It'd been a long time since anyone had cleaned the slats. He'd have to add that to Evans' itinerary.

Chapter 31

Tom lay in bed, wishing for sleep. His digital clock, red numbers in the night, read 2:47 a.m. He'd been watching the time slowly change for the last two hours. Moonlight streamed into the room. It was too bright. He kicked his feet to release his blanket from its tucked in prison at the end of his bed. Too hot. Threw the blanket to the floor. Now, cold. His feet were like ice. No one could sleep with frozen feet.

He leaned over the edge of the bed to grab his blanket from where he had let it fall. His hand found empty space. A cool floor. He flipped over and saw it was in a ball beside his desk. He wondered how it could have gotten that far away from the bed, but in his frustration, anything was possible. At least that was the only explanation he could come up with. Nothing else made sense. He got out of bed, retrieved it and climbed back between his sheets. He punched his pillow, hoping to force it into sleep submission. Make him comfortable, guide him to relaxation. Let him get some damned sleep. He was going to be bleary eyed meeting with Dom tomorrow and he needed to be at his best.

The meeting. The P.O. had practically laughed him off the phone and told him, in no uncertain terms, that it was out of the question. No way, no how, would a meeting between him and Dominic Russell take place. That Mr. Russell had been informed in writing to have no contact with any victim or family member of said victim. Not in public. Not in private. It wasn't done, it wouldn't be done and don't even think of contact through any other source or venue.

Ten minutes later, Bob Walters called back with instructions.

Book a room in the Best Western in Sagerville.

Sagerville. He'd balked at that. It was two hours away, northwest of here. But Walters told him if he wanted the meeting, this was the only thing to which he'd consent. Fine. It had to be in his name, his credit card. This whole "find the foster sister, get rid of her demon" thing was getting expensive for a not-yet-graduated college student. So much for what he'd saved from working at the Penny Saver last summer.

Next, wait in the room. They'd show up; come in separately. Walters would go in first. Make sure things were safe. Private. No listening devices or cameras. Dom would come later. When all was said and done, they'd leave the way they'd arrived, in reverse order. Dom, Walters. Him.

He wanted to bring Stephanie along. After all, she was pretty involved in it now. But he didn't want to push it. Walters already sounded as if he was on the verge of a breakdown, or canceling the meeting altogether. Maybe it was better one on one.

3:07. Minute by minute, this night was going to consume him.

Best Western, Sagerville. All the spots in the parking lot were taken, and he had to drive to the back of the building, into a spare lot, before he found anything. He half expected the girl at the desk to tell him his card was declined or there had been a phone call, a message his friends weren't able to join him. Something to throw a monkey wrench into this day. But no. All was set and confirmed. He had his room keys in hand. 414. A nice round number on an even numbered floor.

He waited in front of the elevator. An out of order sign was hidden behind a potted plant and it took him a minute to realize it was meant for him. "Stairs it is." Not a huge inconvenience. A few flights, whatever. The fire door opened with a thunk, and he took the green cement steps two at a time. They reminded him of dorm stairs.

Generic. Empty, except for those unwilling to squash into the elevator like sardines. No one ever paid attention to the weight or body limit in those things. The dorm elevators always seemed on the verge of collapse.

Second floor landing and up the next flight. Step by step. A window on the outside wall at the landing, next flight.

There was no third-floor door. He looked over the railing, to the second, then back. No door. Odd, but maybe there were odd floor/even floor staircases. It didn't make sense, but who knew what the architect had in mind.

Step, step. Another window. He paused to stare outside. The clouds were rolling in with rain on the horizon. He didn't remember it being in the morning forecast, but the weather app guys couldn't be right all the time. He squinted to see if he could find a rainbow in the distant downpour. Not yet. He'd try from the window in his room. God's promise and all.

There was no door at this landing, either. Did he take a service staircase? No, that would have access to every floor. Maybe this was direct to the roof. He needed to head downstairs, take the correct stairwell or ask the girl at the desk.

The lighting dimmed as he started toward the first floor, the only sound the dull tap of his sneakers on cement. The windows were gone. Pale yellow bulbs in wire covers buzzed in the corners. Step by step. The air grew chillier. A stale breeze wafted from the basement.

He gripped the railing. This wasn't where he had come from. Where was the first-floor door?

There was a fluttering from above.

A knot twisted in his stomach. This couldn't be happening. He turned.

Throughout the stairwell, birds had landed. On the railing, the stairs. Windowsill of the non-existent window.

Crows.

Watching him.

Something told him the only way out was up, and he'd have to pass the birds to do it.

One foot at a time, pushed gently between the birds. He slid past a larger one as it sat rigid, its beak dragging along his shin. The next foot. His sneaker pressing in to slide the bird on the step closer to its mate. Breathe. Slow going. He told himself they were only birds. Nothing to fear. Visions of Alfred Hitchcock's movie played through his mind. Only birds.

He placed his hand on the railing, and the crow sitting there pecked it. He jerked backward, almost losing his footing. Three crows took flight, cawing. It was time to run. His legs pumped, with birds in a flurry around him, cawing, pecking, scratching at him. He batted at them, arms flailing, the skin on his back ripped and shredded by their claws. He saw a door ahead and poured all his energy into reaching it.

Tom slammed the push bar, birds tearing at his arms, and it gave way to the outside. The birds poured out en masse, gliding into the sky.

A figure stood shrouded in a black aura twenty yards away. Olivia.

Tom woke panting. 3:33 a.m.

So little time had passed. Minutes, and yet she was able to send her warning. She knew where he was going. Knew what he was doing.

He rolled over, dragging his blanket to his neck, and winced. Sitting up, he could see in the moonlight welts forming on his forearms.

Chapter 32

Tom balanced his Dunkin' cup, swiped the key and went inside.

He tossed the plastic card onto the computer desk, set the coffee on the windowsill and opened the curtains. Sun poured into the room, lighting the amber carpet and off-white walls. At least it was a nice day. No rain; no birds. Grabbing the remote, he took the corner chair. He was too wound up to relax on the bed. Television on. He skipped to the local news, then to a cartoon channel. He was antsy and bored at the same time, waiting for Russell and Walters to show up. There was nothing to watch. Nothing to do but wait and check the window to see if someone, anyone, had arrived.

He pulled his phone out of his pocket and thumbed through Instagram. Snippets of stupid TikTok videos played, so called "influencers" trying to hit a magic number of followers, of likes, of stupid people believing their staged skits. AI videos with broken hands, unrealistic details. Imperfect teeth. Blurry eyes. Unintelligible text. He liked to scrutinize photos and pick out the mistakes.

Another check out of the window. A glance at the time.

10:55 a.m. Still early. Five long minutes, if they were punctual. More, if they were late. He let out an exasperated sigh, his entire being tense. Tapping his foot against the leg of the chair, he counted the seconds. Maybe he'd had too much caffeine. Or maybe meeting this guy had hyped him a little too much. His nerves were little soldiers, standing at attention. He sipped his coffee. It was still hot. He tapped Google Maps and clicked on Walters' profile under the location share option. The man had him turn it on before they met.

A knock at the door. Tom jumped up, set his coffee on the dresser and opened the door.

"Thomas Anderson?"

An overweight man stood in front of him, round glasses resting on the bridge of his nose. He looked Tom square in the eye.

"Yes," he said. "Mr. Walters?"

"In the flesh."

Tom stepped to the side, holding the door wide. "Come in." He held out his hand.

Walters sidestepped and turned, facing Tom and the door. "If you don't mind, I'll frisk you first."

"Excuse me?"

"I'm here to make sure Dom is safe and you are what you say you are. I'm going to pat you down and then examine the room for any possible weapons or bugs."

"Uh, sure. That would be fine."

Walters motioned him forward, then proceeded to frisk him from head to arms, waist band to legs.

"Do I need to take off my shoes?"

"I'm not with the TSA," Walters said. "Besides if you go for your shoe while I'm here, know that I am faster with this," he touched his gun, "than you could ever be with that."

Tom smiled nervously. "Of that, I'm sure."

Walters unzipped his brown canvas jacket and laid it across the back of the desk chair. "If you'll bear with me a few minutes, I have a job to do."

Tom gave him the go ahead with a wave of his arm and sat in the chair by the window. He watched as the man surveyed the room: wires, underneath the bed, behind the headboard, around the outlets and the sprinkler system. The television. Opening the closet, he tapped the panels and then went into the bathroom. A few minutes later, he was done.

"Things seem to check out." He peered at the room, in

thought, then pulled the desk to an open area away from the windows. "Close the blinds. I'll call Dom."

"Thank you." Tom did as he asked and clicked on the lamp, but when Walters said "Dom," all he could picture were ball gags and whips. He squeezed his eyes shut. The stress was getting to him. Anxiety was ran through his veins, Something had to give soon.

"Yeah, yeah. Okay," Walters said into a flip phone. "Okay." He snapped the burner shut. "He's on his way up."

Dom walked into the room and Walters deadbolted the door, then swing latched it and taped over the peep hole.

Tom was like a nervous kid. "Mr. Russell." He extended his hand. "I'm really glad you came."

Dom regarded him for a moment, hung his glasses on the neckband of his shirt and shook his hand. "Tom."

"Please, have a seat." He motioned to the computer desk where he'd placed two straight backed chairs, one on either side. Walters took the comfortable seat in the corner, where he could keep an eye on them.

Dom hooked his cane onto the edge of the desk and sat. He ran a hand through his greying hair. Tom slid into the seat facing him.

"Well?" Dom said. "You asked me to come. Here I am."

"It's hard to know where to start." Actually, it was damned near impossible. The thousand questions he had for the man stuck in his throat, all struggling to be asked, all unable to escape his lips.

"Your girlfriend said you were the little boy at the house when everything went south."

"I was."

Dom braced his feet on the floor and leaned backward, stretching his back. "Sorry to hear that."

"Thanks." He rested his hands on the desk, adjusting the little pile of hotel note pads, and the pen beside them. He sucked up his courage. "Why did you go to Wyoming?"

Walters bristled, lips a thin line, but stayed out of the conversation. He still wasn't thrilled he had been coerced into making that happen. And how did the kid know?

Dom glanced at his P.O. His friend. The truth was all he had, and he hoped Bob could handle it. "I was tracking Olivia." Sheepishly, he said, "Sorry, Bob."

Walters sighed.

"Why did you try to kill her? Twenty years ago. Why did you go after her?"

Dom narrowed his eyes. The trial, reporters, years of finger pointing and questions and here it was all over again. "Look. Your little girlfriend said that there were bad things happening and you called me here. I assume you know the answer to your own question."

"A lot of old memories have been surfacing. My time at that house, and before. When I lived beside Amanda. Of," he swallowed, "Black."

Dom folded his arms across his chest. "Right."

"I always thought going into the ministry was because I had a calling. A closeness to God. But now I think I was scared. In need of protection. And didn't know why." He looked at Dom, Walters. "I graduate next week."

"Congratulations."

He cleared his throat. "But these memories. I started putting the pieces together. I was mixed up with that thing at the time and didn't know it. Didn't know what it was. Or what it had done. I realized it dropped me for Olivia. I flew out to her grandmother's for answers, too. To find out where she was. See if that thing was still in her or if it's moved on. I went to talk with her. Her soul's in danger. Something has to be done."

Dom unfolded his arms, leaned closer. "Her soul is gone."

"No. I don't believe that."

"She sold it decades ago."

"If she's possessed. We can help her."

"You really don't understand what we're dealing with."

Tom was incredulous. "I know better than anyone."

"Look." Dom put his palms on the desk. "I've been fighting this a lot longer than you. It killed who knows how many people, including two of my friends, and stole the last twenty years of my life."

"You think I don't know what it's capable of? I lived with it. Was taken in by it." He stood, pacing in the small space between the desk and the window.

Walters tensed.

"It killed my mother! It made me kill Amanda!"

Dom leaped to his feet, knocking his chair over, hands balled into fists. "You."

Walters' hand went to his gun. Instincts on alert, he hoped he didn't have to use it. There'd be no explaining that one. They'd all be in prison. "Dom!" he hissed.

Tom locked eyes with the man he'd called for help.

Dom breathed slowly, working his fists, then cracked his knuckles. "Not you," he said. "It. It killed Amanda."

"I'm sorry," Tom said. He looked at the floor. "I didn't even remember that until last week. I was only five."

Dom righted his chair.

"Sorry," Tom said in a hushed tone. "Sorry."

"It wasn't you. Or your fault. My reaction was . . ." There was no word, no explanation. It was pure emotion for his friend. Pure hatred for the demon. "A reaction."

"I found Olivia. Went to see her. She's at-"

"The old asylum."

He nodded. "Forest View. But while I was in Wyoming, my girlfriend went to Olivia's house. She and her friend wanted to do an EVP session, a mini investigation, in the backyard where Seth died."

Dom rolled his eyes. Of course they had. Kids never knew

when to leave things alone.

"Olivia was there. They did something with the Ouija board. Steph said there was a scream and Seth's spirit was gone."

"She's in deep. She's actively working for him, stealing souls."

"I went to see her."

"Not your best idea."

"She's got these people there. Expressionless. With the odor of decomposition."

"Death."

"Yes."

"Shells of people. Bodies with no substance except decay. She's messing with necromancy."

"But that's not possible." He knew he was wrong when it left his lips. More things in heaven and earth, yet again. "But why?" Tom couldn't wrap his mind around it all.

"Loyalty. To the death. Followers who do her bidding. It's control and she's stocking the place to make it harder for anyone to get in and dispose of the demon. It's giving her 'gifts' in return for the souls she takes."

"She bragged about the things she could do."

"There you go."

They were quiet for a moment when Dom stood. He held out his hand.

"Thank you. I appreciate the information. It'll definitely give me direction in what I need to do."

Tom took his hand, then dropped it. "Wait, what? This isn't just your vendetta. That mantle was thrust on me a long time ago. I think we need to work together on this."

"You're not ready." Dom dismissed him, picked up his cane.

From the corner of the room, Walters said, "What do you mean, what you need to do?"

Dom ignored him.

"Look, I'm a minister. I figure an exorcism needs to be done to free Olivia and I'm going to do it."

"She's past that. The entire property would need to be exorcised." Dom waved him off, shaking his head. "Don't even think about it. You're too inexperienced. You'd make things worse."

"Go to hell."

"I believe the expression is, I'm already there. I have nothing to lose. You have your entire life ahead of you."

"And I've been touched by this thing. How long do you think that life will be?"

Dom knew he was right. Once the demon entered your life, everything was tainted.

Outside their window, a crow cawed. Tom startled, giving a quick look over his shoulder. The blinds were still closed, curtains drawn. Dom raised an eyebrow.

"Sounded like it was right outside." Tom's voice was tense.

"I'm sure it was." He inhaled, then exhaled slowly. "You don't see the grand scheme of things. This isn't a grumpy spirit bent on bothering the crap out of people, kicking them out of its house. This is huge. Generations long. Hell, likely longer than even that." He hooked his cane once more and grabbed the chair.

"Look, I'm on edge. I didn't sleep well last night. A cross between insomnia and a nightmare. Kind of ridiculous, right?" He glanced at Walters. Dom.

"Last night an outlet in my bedroom caught fire. Some electrical thing. It was the outlet where I charge my phone."

"Okay." Tom picked up a pen, absently running his thumb along its pocket clip.

"This is after the first two halfway houses that I was assigned to burned to the ground."

"Weird coincidence."

Another raise of an eyebrow. He scoffed. "A warning. There are no coincidences." He sat forward. "What was your nightmare?"

Tom told him. The stairwell, the darkness. The birds. Olivia.

"I'd say we're being told to back off."

A mounting anxiety grew Tom's chest. His underarms were damp and staining his shirt.

Dom wanted to do this alone. Not involve anyone else the way he'd brought in Amanda. But the kid was right. Black would be after him the rest of his days, and they were both in his line of sight.

"So, perhaps we should combine forces."

Tom agreed. "What's the plan?"

While they talked, Walters left the room. He didn't want to know about exorcisms or plans or anything else that was involved. Plausible deniability. And he was going to need all that he could possibly get.

Chapter 33

It was late as Reilly approached his room. Another night of grave digging, another body raised into Olivia's arsenal. He was dirty, sweaty and his back ached. He rolled his neck in an arc, stretching the muscles. It cracked. All he wanted was to get into bed and sleep for days.

But he heard something. Shuffling. Things being moved. He deftly slid the key into the lock, flung open the door and hit the lights.

Morts. The Morts were in his apartment, and all his things were in disarray. Cushions off the sofa, end table drawers hanging open. Vince looked up at him and went back to digging through a cabinet.

"What the hell are you doing?"

He strode to the dead man and shoved him out of the way, then saw that Margaret was in his kitchen. "What the fuck's going on in here?" He ran from room to room. They were everywhere. A Mort in the bathroom, one in the bedroom rummaging through his closet. "Out! Out!" He grabbed the bathroom one by the arm. Tony, he thought. As if it mattered. They ceased having identities when they died. A Mort was a Mort was a Mort.

It pulled away from him with strength he hadn't anticipated and went back to what it was doing.

"The fuck!"

He grabbed clothes off the floor, stuffing them into drawers, and noticed one of his sneakers was missing. On hands and knees, he looked under the bed, then pawed through his closet. Open boxes fell around him. It was gone.

Enough was enough. Olivia had explaining to do. He ran to

the basement, through her office and barged into her apartment. "Olivia!"

A voice came from the bathroom where he could hear the shower running. "Just a minute." There was a sweet sing-song lilt in her voice. He knew better. She was well aware why he was there. He was sure of it. His arms were crossed and his foot tapped angrily.

She emerged wrapped in a towel, hair swept up in another. If she were any other woman or he wasn't mad as a bull in a bullfight, he'd have been on her before the towels hit the floor. But this was too much.

"Why the hell are your baboons in my apartment?!"

She smiled. "You're one of my baboons."

"No!" He shoved a recliner, almost tipping it over. "I'm not. I am so much more than they are. I've got a soul."

Olivia stared him down, hands on her hips.

"Why?" he asked.

She shrugged. "Seemed appropriate. Necessary. You've been having some issues with the demands of the job. Grumbling at my requests on your time." She pulled the towel from her hair. "Oh, Brutus. I need to know everything is safe. Secure. I'd hate for you to be harboring weapons or thinking that you'd, I don't know, try to take me out one day. Knock me off. Be top dog or something. You've had a wild hair up your ass for a while now."

"It's my apartment."

"Consider it keeping you on your toes. I'm going to need you at your best soon, chop chop and all that. Things here may get a little nasty, but it's nothing we can't handle together. I have to be certain you're not packing to leave. I'd have to find someone to fill your shoes. That would suck for both of us. Yes?" She fluffed her hair with the towel, then tossed it over the back of a chair.

"Yes." Yes, because he'd either be dead and risen again as a Mort or taken away in a straitjacket. "But if you know my thoughts, you should know I'm not going anywhere."

She scoffed. "I can't read your mind. Just little things here and there. I'm not omniscient." She paused. "Yet."

"Will you get them out of there so I can get some sleep?"

She regarded him for a moment, then seemed to focus on a point far behind him. "They're out."

He sighed. "Thank you." He hated having to express gratitude for something that shouldn't have been in the first place. Didn't like thanking her when what he wanted to do was scream. It left a vile taste in his mouth.

"They stole one of my sneakers."

Olivia clamped a hand over her mouth to suppress her laughter. "They what?"

"You heard me. One of my sneakers is gone."

She waved him off. "Go, go. I'll put a little something in your pay this week to cover a new pair. And get a shower. You're pretty ripe."

Reilly scowled, then nodded, turning.

"Close the door on your way out."

Chapter 34

Tom sat at his desk, right hand hovering in front of the printer as the next page rolled out. He placed it on top of the stack and went back to the computer screen. His Bible lay open at the keyboard, empty Dunkin' cups to the side. The printer whirred to life once more. Stephanie sat on the bed, laptop on her knees.

"Printing the prayer to Archangel Michael."

"Great," Tom said. "That was next on my list. Printing Psalm 91."

Tom was thumbing through his Bible, searching for the next verse he wanted, when Paul strode in sporting a Pantera sweatshirt.

"Hey, happy people! Two days till graduation. How's it hanging, Rev.?" He clapped his friend on the back.

"Good, good. What's doing on your side of the campus?" Tom swiveled the chair to face him.

Stephanie waved hello and set her laptop on the pillow.

"There's a party brewing."

"When's there not?" Tom laughed.

"It's the last hurrah before we get ordained. Lots of little ministers will be pouring out of here on Saturday, ready to take on the spiritual world. Got to exorcise the last of our demons with comradery, alcohol and maybe some debauchery."

Stephanie threw a balled-up piece of paper at him, hitting him in the stomach. "How does debauchery get rid of demons? Isn't that quite the opposite of spirituality?"

"Hmm," he said. "Picture it like a bachelor party. The bachelor isn't getting rid of his fiancé or canceling the wedding. He's having some fun, sowing a wild oat or two."

She shook her head. "Nope. Wild oats are not acceptable."

"To each his own." He turned to Tom. "You in?"

Another paper ball flew past his head.

"Sorry, man. Can't. Not only do I have a ball and chain," he inclined his head toward Stephanie, "but I'll be busy the next couple of days."

Paul furrowed his brow. "Days? What's doing?" He took the paper sitting in the printer output tray. "'The prayer to Archangel Michael?" He tossed it on Tom's desk. "1 Timothy 4:1? Tell me you're putting together a sermon, or some weird religious version of Dungeons and Dragons, and you're not planning an exorcism on that girl." He saw an insulated lunch bag tucked under Tom's desk with small bottles of liquid in it.

Tom gathered the empty coffee cups and tossed them into the trash. "It's decided."

"Is that what I think it is?" He nudged the bag with his foot.

"It is. Holy water. Made it myself."

"You're doing this."

"Yes."

Paul glanced at Stephanie, eyes raised as if to ask, "You're letting him?" Then back to Tom. "You're not qualified."

"I'm on the side of good. I have God with me. What more do I need?"

"Knowledge. Experience. You'll get thrown out of the ministry. Leave it to the Catholics. They have priests trained for this."

"That's too long a process. They have to examine, decide if mental illness is involved, and so on."

"For good reason!" He slapped his arms to his sides.

"We need to act, Paul."

"What about graduation? Are you going to miss that?"

"Are you seriously putting a cap and gown celebration above someone's soul?" They were face to face, chest to chest.

Paul shook his head. "I'm not convinced she's at risk, man."

"I am."

Paul rested his fingertips on the back of Tom's computer chair. He spun it, catching it on the third circle around.

"I think you're in too deep." He stared at his friend, concerned with more than his mental health. More than his decision making. "And if you're right? If she's possessed, truly taken over by something demonic?"

"I was going to ask if you'd help us."

Paul met Tom's eyes, searching for something he could reason with. Connect with. "No. I can't get behind it."

Tom was disappointed, but it was the answer he expected. "I understand," he said. "And I'm sorry, Paul, but you need to leave. We have preparations to make."

His friend was frozen in place for a moment, then said, "Later, man," and walked out the door.

"Wow." Stephanie's jaw dropped.

"It's okay," Tom said. "We'll be okay."

"What if we're not?"

"Hm?" He had gotten lost in his own thoughts of what might happen that day. He'd hoped Paul would join them. Help. Every voice in prayer could only add to the strength of their convictions. To the ability to end this thing.

The door opened. They looked up to see Paul, visibly upset. Rattled. "If you're right. If this does go down the way you think it might, remember Ephesians 6."

"Paul."

"Ephesians 6." His demeanor, deeply serious. Eyes wide. This wasn't the joking, Black Sabbath wearing boy who ate pizza and talked sex. This was a man coming to his aid the only way he felt he could. He walked out as quickly as he'd come in.

Stephanie picked up the Bible beside her. "Ephesians 6?"

Tom looked into her eyes. "Verse 6. Put on the full armor of

God."

They were silent for a moment, and Stephanie asked, "Tom, what if the exorcism doesn't work? How much trouble are we in?"

It was a terrifying prospect and one he didn't want to explore. "There's always a plan B."

"And that is?"

He turned toward his computer. "I'm working on it."

Chapter 35

Olivia stood in her bedroom doorway. It'd been a long day. Issues with Brutus, *Reilly*, as he liked to remind her. As if she forgot. She just didn't care and enjoyed making him cringe. And his biggest worries were the Morts in his room and a missing sneaker. He was a coward in brute's clothing. She smirked. A doer of dirty work. A doer of . . . she thought back to the afternoon on the sofa with him and a soft tingling between her legs remembered the encounter. A momentary lapse, but worth it.

She looked around the room and sighed. She hadn't paid much attention to things like laundry or picking up. The hamper beside the bathroom door was overflowing. Too much time in the cemeteries. Even with Brutus doing all the grunt work, a girl still got dirty. Or maybe it was dealing with the newly deceased. Either way, she'd have one of the Morts take care of it in the morning. Someone had to.

She drew back her comforter and sheet, tossing the throw pillows to the floor. A room done in shades of lavender that she was rarely in. She slid off her slippers and climbed between the covers. They were cool and crisp. Inviting. Taking off her glasses, she set them on the night table and switched off the light. Another day in the books, more Morts in her collection. Her personal legion, if Black let her keep them.

She pulled the blankets up to her chin. She liked to sleep in a chilly room, and the fact that her apartment butted up against Black's sanctuary was not only comforting, but downright cold as he came and went.

But then there was Tommy.

Her mood darkened. She wondered if he had the balls to return and challenge her. Challenge *him*. It'd be his undoing if he tried. Reverend, my ass, she thought. Another coward hiding behind religion. Shaking in his shoes.

And Dom. Ever present. Ever involved. That washed up, wanna-be ghost hunting demon slayer. She chuckled. The two of them together couldn't take her, let alone Black. She doubted they could even get past the Morts.

A wintry breeze passed through her room, and she shivered before drifting off to sleep.

Chapter 36

Dom and his counselor sat across from each other in a Second Chance side room. It was a redone bedroom, by the look of it. Sofa on the longer wall, overstuffed armchairs. Inspirational posters adorning the walls. All in shades of peach and brown. It felt more like a girl's bedroom than anything else. Dom could picture teen girls painting their nails and chatting about boys there. Maybe the powers that be should have considered the population they were trying to service when they decorated the room.

His counselor spoke. "Bob Walters tells me you're interested in pursuing retirement rather than returning to the workforce."

"That's right." Retirement. From the frying pan into the fire was more like it. Demon hunting at its finest, with the bastard in his sights.

"That's fine and Bob will certainly be working with you on that end of things. You know, social security, Medicare, things like that. But what we need to figure out is how you'll be spending your days. You need things to fill the hours, give you a sense of fulfillment at the end of the day. Satisfaction. Have you thought about volunteering anywhere? Or taking continuing education courses? I want to help you capitalize on your interests. Help you move forward. Your past doesn't define you. Your present does. You need to become the person you were always meant to be."

The man was wrong. His past did define him. It defined his days and nights and had become a singular focus. He was going to spend his remaining days on earth going after a demon. This was his time. "I would like to take some classes."

"Wonderful. Let's go through the NCC catalog and get some ideas for the summer."

He didn't tell the guy that this was his last day at Second Chance. When they heard his name again, he'd be on his way back to prison. Or dead. The jury was out.

The day wore on. After the evening routine, the men retired to their rooms for designated quiet hours. Dom pulled a book off the shelf in the hall and brought it with him. Propping up on his pillows, he laid the book open to his side and waited for the head count.

Someone knocked on his door. Alan Evans stuck in his head. "How's it going, Dominic?"

"Good." He motioned with the book.

"What are you reading?" Evans did the obligatory one-foot step inside the room, not meaning to get into a real conversation.

Dom held it up. To Evans, the red cover said it all.

"Man's Search for Meaning. Great book." He put his hand on his chest. "Let me know what you think of it."

"For sure."

"Good man. Have a good night. See you at group in the morning."

Evans stepped out, closing the door behind him. Dom let the book drop. He had other things on his mind.

Pulling some weights from under the bed, he began bicep curls. He didn't want to lose the strength he'd gained in prison.

He lay awake, waiting for the minutes to tick by. All his preparations were in place. He wouldn't lose this time. His heartbeat kept pace with the clock on the wall. Controlled. Steady. No need to rush. He'd had twenty-two years to get this right. No turning back. No second, third or fourth chances. But he wouldn't need more than one.

1:15 a.m.

He heard them come for the curfew count at 12:30 a.m. and pretended to be asleep. They looked in, satisfied, and went to the next door. He'd be long gone before they checked again.

Dom rolled out of bed. His clothes were laid out on the chair. Black pants, black tee. Belt. He put on his sneakers, then went to the closet to get his bag and dumped the contents onto the bed. Tactical combat knife. Saged, blessed and ready for action. Cans of hairspray, a handful of lighters. Damn, it was good to have a friend on the inside. Someone who could get him what he needed without Alan Evans, Director, finding out. Rah, rah, Evans. Go team.

He reached into the bottom of the bag and smiled. His chess set. He'd made it over the last few months in the prison wood shop, infusing every piece with his intent. His focus. His desire to destroy the demon who'd crashed through his life. His hatred. Flipping it over, his fingers traced the letters he'd burned into the wood. A crude alphabet with a yes and no at the corners. An energy ran from the board through his fingertips.

"Not yet, my friend. Not yet."

It had finally clicked as he sat to rot in Aarondale Correctional. If you wanted to annihilate a demon, you had to think like a demon. If you wanted to save souls, you'd have to give up your own. This was it. Endgame for Black.

He attached the knife to his belt. Evans' car keys were the last thing in the bag. Dom stuffed everything into a small backpack. Without his cane. Since he started working with the other side, his leg had slowly healed. Bones shattered twenty-five years ago were strong.

He was ready for war.

Chapter 37

They parked in different areas. Dom left Evans' car behind the Salvation Army building, the farthest spot under the cover of some trees. It would be hours before the car was noticed missing and more before they'd find it here. A sign on the far fence said that violators would be towed. That was fine with him.

Tom chose the lot beside the Methodist Church on Frontier Street and Stephanie was at the Dunkin' on Main. It was closed, the only light coming from streetlights and a dull spotlight on the cash register inside. Dom hadn't wanted to draw attention. Three cars parked together when everything was closed for the night was not good. And pulling up the Forest View drive together wouldn't only bring the cops, it would be three energies combined that Black would be watching. Separately, they might have a little more time before being noticed.

Dom walked up to Stephanie's car and tapped on the driver's side window. She rolled it down. Tom was in the passenger side with a thermos of coffee.

"Are you ready?"

"I don't know if I'll ever be ready," Stephanie responded.

"Then you shouldn't be here."

"What I meant was-"

Tom put his hand on her knee. "We're ready."

"We go in separately. One up the drive, the other two from the woods. We'll meet at the north end of the building at the far apartment. Be aware of your surroundings. Do you have everything you're going to need?" He held up his pack for emphasis. "There's no coming back in the middle of things."

"Yes, of course." Tom picked up his container of vials, and his Bible.

Stephanie wore a necklace with a silver cross, matching Tom's. "I hope it's enough."

"You have to be confident. Believe in what you're doing. And, no matter what, have each other's back."

Tom nodded. "What's in the bag?"

"Insurance." He turned. "Some weapons. We need to get moving. If we waste too much time, they'll be ready for us."

Tom pulled on the door handle. "Let's go."

"And remember. When we're inside, I take point. I've been here before."

Somehow, to Tom, that wasn't comforting.

Stephanie walked up the drive. She thought taking it would be the better choice, letting the men traipse through the woods, but regretted her decision. This was intimidating. Everywhere she looked there were shadows. Tricks of the light, sure, but her paranormal senses were heightened. Every snap of a twig had her on edge. Her hands clenched into fists when, out of nowhere, a howling began. Small, distant, but growing louder and echoing. A pack of coyotes on the prowl and making the night feel much more dangerous. She strode on, wishing Tom was beside her.

She kept close to the bushes that lined the drive, hoping she could shield herself, blend in, as long as possible. She hadn't thought about the fact that she'd have the longest walk out in the open, across the lot to the edge of the building. A light burned in the front lobby. If she kept to the tree line as long as she could, things might be okay. She kept her eyes low, watching the moonlit ground to avoid looking at the windows. The night was creepy enough; she didn't want to see anything watching her. She could feel the energy inherent in this place . . . Forest View, aka New Castle Asylum . . . and it was bleak. Disturbing. Looming. She focused on moving forward and shut out the rest.

Dom circled from the southeast, up the eastern side and slowly made his way across tree roots and bushes, ducking branches. It was the longest way to where they would meet, but he needed to be the farthest. The most under the radar. The cargo he carried, his arsenal, couldn't be discovered until he was ready. At least the reverend's exorcism would be a distraction.

Chapter 38

Brian slipped his fingers under the toe of the sneaker, channeling his energy. His focus. He flipped it. His mind surged with excitement. His abilities were expanding, getting stronger, and his practice was paying off.

He tried again. Flip. He jumped. Fist pumped the air.

Everything was better since he discovered he could bring objects back to his room. The things he found. He didn't need to be in room 104, rushing out whenever Olivia's flunky returned. It happened one day with the penny. He'd had his finger on it when he heard the key in the lock of the door. He dematerialized, blipped out, whatever you called his disappearing act, and when he was back in his own room, the penny fell to the floor. He'd stared at it, trying to comprehend what had happened. Being able to bring something back with him even though he wasn't able to lift it. That soon changed.

And he practiced day and night.

Next would be lifting the shoe. Then, something bigger. He didn't know what. What he did know was that this would be the thing that saved him. The thing that would keep him from being annihilated by Black.

He looked at the small clock he'd brought back to the room. Luckily, it was battery operated since he hadn't been able to lift a plug or shove one into an outlet. 2:58 a.m. The asylum was asleep. But out the window, a shadow caught his attention. It blended with the trees and, for a moment, he thought he was mistaken.

It shifted again. A person.

And it was headed toward Forest View.

231

Chapter 39

Tom squatted behind a bush, keeping an eye on the woods and building, his jaw aching. He hadn't even noticed how hard he'd been clenching it. Every muscle in his body was tense. Tight with adrenalin. In the moonlight he could see his hands trembling. A small hangnail on his thumb caught his attention and he brought it to his mouth. He chewed on it as he waited for Dom to get to his position.

His cellphone vibrated. Pulling it from his jacket pocket, the screen lit his face. Bob Walters. He sent it to voicemail. As he shut the phone off, he saw that the hangnail had torn up the side of his thumb, almost to the knuckle, a bead of blood welling up. It stung as he sucked at it, watching. Waiting.

Stephanie crouched by the last apartment on the north side of the building. This was nothing like going into an investigation, nothing she ever thought she'd experience in her lifetime. Or wanted to. And yet something led her here. Something more than her relationship with Tom or the paranormal. She had a momentary existential pause; there was no time for a crisis. She stayed low, hoping nothing noticed her. Hoping they'd all walk out together when it was done. Whole. Safe.

She pulled off a glove and reached into the back pocket of her jeans. Her recorder. She clicked it to on, then clipped it onto a chain on her beltloop. Whatever came from tonight, she'd have a record. Documentation. Something to show the world, or maybe to prove to themselves, what happened. What they went through.

She waited, nerves on edge, for the men to come from the woods.

When Tom saw Dom break the tree line, he made a beeline for the building and, as they approached, Stephanie stood.

"Did you hear those coyotes?" she asked, voice low.

"One more thing sent to distract us. Scare us away," Dom said.

She rubbed her hands together, the chill of the night seeping through her knit gloves. "You think so?"

"Easily could be. Someone else might have turned away, gone back to the cars." He looked around, taking stock of their surroundings. "It's not going to be that easy." He dropped his pack to the ground, took out a small tool and wedged it into the lock of the sliding glass door of the apartment. Three seconds went by. Four. Click. He slid the door to the side, and they went in.

"That was slick," Stephanie whispered. "You'd think it'd harder to get inside."

"With age comes wisdom. And burglary tools," Dom said, grabbing his pack. "We may have to fight our way to the basement." He handed Stephanie the hairspray and lighters, unsheathed his knife. "I'll go first. Tom, you stay between us. I'll incapacitate and Stephanie will burn whatever doesn't stay down. You hit them with that holy water as we go."

Tom tucked his Bible into the pocket of his bag and slung the strap around his neck. Unzipping his waist pack, he picked up the first vial.

"Let's do this."

Chapter 40

The temperature in her room dropped and Olivia startled awake. Something felt off. Wrong. She fumbled for her glasses and checked her phone for the time. 3:00 a.m. Realization sunk in as her brain woke.

"Son of a bitch," she said. "They're here."

Anger filled her. She hadn't been asleep long and here they were, throwing a monkey wrench into the works. Trying to ruin her plans. Demolish her empire! The hubris! The utter balls they had to go after her, and they thought they could win against Black.

They were an infuriating nuisance, and she was done. They'd been a game, a toy. An annoying mosquito that kept returning, swatted away and still back droning in her ear. This would end tonight. *They would end tonight.* How dare that little boy think he could take her down.

Throwing off the covers, she focused on the Morts, sending one message. *Give them hell.*

She would be ready. And waiting.

Chapter 41

Dom put his ear to the door and listened. There was movement in the hallway. Footsteps, muffled by the indoor-outdoor carpet these places seemed to favor. He motioned to Tom and Stephanie that they weren't alone and held his knife in front of him as he slowly unlocked the deadbolt. At the click of its release, the movement halted.

He held his breath.

After what seemed like minutes, the shuffling resumed. A click echoed. The footsteps moved into the living quarters to their left.

"They must be checking each of the rooms," he whispered. "That's good for us."

"How so?" Stephanie asked.

"Tom and I will hang farther back. By the windows. You wait behind the door. When they enter, they'll come toward us. We hit them from the front, and you get them from behind."

"We don't even know who it is."

Dom looked her straight in the eyes. "We do. Entirely. They're either alive or something Olivia has raised from the dead. Either way, they'll be willing to kill to get us out of here."

"I-"

"This isn't the time. If you're not committed, leave. You can get out the way we came in. Just decide where you stand. And do it now." He tossed his backpack onto the bed.

Stephanie looked to Tom, who agreed. "This is it, Steph. There's only one way forward for me. You can go if you need to. This isn't going to be easy."

She took her place behind the door, hairspray and lighter at the ready.

Tom untwisted the top on a vial of holy water. He positioned himself across from Dom, the sliding door at their backs, and waited for the knob to turn.

The smell hit Stephanie first. Worse than when a skunk wandered into her basement and died behind some tires. This was decay and chemical bile boiled on a stove. Inhuman. She covered her nose with the back of her hand as the door opened.

A woman and two men filed into the room. The woman saw them first. The two flanked her.

"Vince, Garret. Take them down." She took a step backward to block the way out.

"So," Dom said. "You're what passes as flesh these days? Pitiful." He brandished the knife in front of him.

Vince sneered, pushing a shock of hair off his forehead, revealing cracks in his skin. "You won't have to smell it long." He lunged at Dom, who met him halfway, stabbing him in the stomach. A yellow-green goo poured from the wound. The thing went to its knees as Dom yanked the knife back.

Garret dove for Tom.

Stephanie stepped from the doorway and yelled, "Tom! Get down!"

The two corpses turned. Stephanie squeezed the button on the hairspray and aimed it over the flame of the lighter. The blowtorch sprayed across their faces, melting flesh and releasing the rest of the caustic chemicals inside their rotting bodies. Blisters bubbled and popped across their flesh.

"Good job, Steph," Dom said. "Ease off, though. Don't use all your spray on these. There'll be plenty more as we go."

She stood over the spasming bodies. Tom gagged. He fumbled with the vial, almost dropping it, then made the sign of the cross across them with the holy water.

"Hold it together, Rev. We're far from done."

The bodies fell quiet, their juddering over.

"Should you, I mean, do you need to cut off their heads or something?" Stephanie poked one with the toe of her shoe. Its head lolled to the side, dead eyes staring at nothing. Foam rose where the holy water had touched its skin.

"I will," Dom said. "For good measure." The truth was, he wasn't sure if the trauma they'd inflicted was enough or if the heads should come off. It depended on how strong Olivia's necromancy had become.

"Did you notice this?" Stephanie used her foot again to point out a crow tattoo on the woman's wrist. "All three of them have it."

Dom leaned closer. "It must bind them together. Olivia probably has one, too. Something that ties her to these things." He held the knife over Vince's neck.

Stephanie turned away and Tom escorted her to the doorway. After a couple of quick slices, Dom slung his backpack onto his back and joined them.

"We need to move carefully. Alert. Focused. Don't let one of these things get the better of you with the element of surprise." He wiped his knife off on his pants. "And some may be harder to kill than others. Those with less decomposition than these guys," he blew air out of his nose to try to clear the odor, "will likely be tougher."

His cohorts nodded.

"Are we ready?"

Curt nods.

They left the room.

There were footsteps in the lobby. Dom flattened against the wall, with Stephanie and Tom following suit opposite him. They moved in unison, inching toward the end of the hallway.

A man rushed them, trying to grab Dom by the throat. Dom countered with an uppercut of the knife, catching the corpse under its chin. The knife plunged into the soft palate and stuck. The dead man, more a bloated hotdog than a person, grabbed at his face, pawing for the knife. They both took hold and pulled, but Dom had the tighter grip. He got a handful of the thing's hair, yanked its head back and sliced its throat. Bile yellow maggots spilled out, climbing through a brown crust.

Another corpse came from behind, seizing Dom's pack and twisting it, tightening the straps like a noose around his neck. He dropped the knife as his hands dug at the strap, trying to work his fingers beneath it.

"Go!" Stephanie yelled.

Tom stepped to the side as she moved forward, aiming a can of hairspray at the thing choking Dom. She flicked the lighter and sprayed a short burst at the dead man's back.

It dropped the pack.

Dom whipped the pack off, scooped up the knife and shoved it into the thing's stomach. A gurgling sound, bubbly and thick, escaped its mouth as its body shuddered and slumped to the floor. Lifeless. Deathless. Embalming fluid mixed with decaying liquids dripped from the gaping wound.

Tom held his breath, making the sign of the cross with the holy water across its chest.

Dom rubbed his neck. A red welt rose where the strap had threatened to cut off his airway.

Another down.

Three more coming.

Tom's legs went weak. He clutched his bag and prayed as they fought their way toward the stairwell. Five down. Six.

Seven.

# # #

Reilly heard muffled voices outside his door. A commotion. He'd taken to sleeping fully dressed, with life at Forest View so unpredictable. Sleeping naked didn't work if the Morts were going to come and go as they pleased. As *she* pleased. And he had to be ready at a moment's call if Olivia needed him. It made things easier.

And he'd gotten her text. "Get down here."

He guessed this was what she meant by things getting nasty. He walked into the bathroom and stared at his reflection in the mirror. He'd grown older in the last few months. Digging up the dead. Watching her rip apart spirits. He reached into the toilet tank for a compartment the Morts hadn't known about. Hadn't found. He'd watched The Godfather. Knew a little about keeping things hidden if he had to. The 40 caliber Glock 22 was where he'd hidden it. He loaded it and stepped into his living room.

Everything quieted as the footsteps moved toward the basement. They must've gotten through these Morts. But there were some in every hallway with guards at her office.

They were at a crossroads. A showdown.

It was time to act. Kill or be killed.

Chapter 42

They regrouped at the stairwell in the corner of the lobby. Tom didn't know how many of the undead they'd killed. He was sweating. Unnerved. Evil was present here in ways he hadn't imagined. A year ago, he'd been happily in denial; memories tightly boxed up and shoved away. Yet something in him remembered. Had known what he'd be up against. Something pushed him into the ministry, showing him the path to defeat this festering unholy darkness.

Nothing he'd studied at seminary prepared him for this.

Burned, rotting corpses littered the lobby. Throats slit, stomachs sliced.

Stephanie shook the can in her hand, then tossed it to the floor. She pulled the next from her bag. Dom cleaned his knife off on a curtain, smearing a dark sticky fluid across it. No one would be coming in to rent apartments here for a very long time.

A third of Tom's vials were empty. He set them on a table.

Dom waited at the door to the basement. "Things will get harder from here. There are probably more of those things. And then there's Olivia."

"You're sure she'll be here?"

"She has no reason to hide. We've been warned to stay away, yet here we are. She'll be waiting."

Tom's mouth was dry. "And either victory, or else a grave."

"Macbeth?" Stephanie asked.

"Henry VI."

Dom shoved open the door.

A rush of wings and the roar of screaming caws caused Tom

to flail and jump backward, slamming into the wall. Stephanie ducked, hands over her head. Only Dom stood tall. He'd expected the fight to escalate. Rise to another level. Prey on their fear. The reanimated dead were a small obstacle. A speed bump. Olivia would do almost anything to keep them out, and Black would do even more.

He knew from his nightmares the terror that could be inflicted on an unprepared mind. He was ready. He hoped the reverend and his girl were. Either way, he was in it till the end. Whatever that end would be.

The stairwell was empty.

They started down. Dom had worked long and hard to prepare himself for the flood of memories this building held for him. Joking with Amanda while setting up basecamp. Brian always having a snappy comeback. He frowned. Of the caretaker, Joe Paine, and how Black had possessed him. Tried to kill them all. Of how they'd lost Brian, and he'd been maimed. It worked for the most part. He channeled his pain into purpose. He'd get Black this time.

Stephanie matched steps with him. "Didn't you have a limp? You were walking with a cane when we met."

He smiled in the dim light, shifting the pack across his shoulders. "I've gotten better."

Tom recovered, counted the remaining vials, and followed Stephanie. It didn't take long to catch up as they reached the bottom. Dom took a breath.

The door ahead creaked open and scraped across the concrete floor, like an old hospital fire door.

No one noticed Reilly at the top of the steps behind them.

Dom inclined his head and pointed with the knife. "I'm assuming that's where she'll be. The office," he whispered. "The old morgue."

Two corpses stood guard, one on either side of the entrance. The closest looked as if he could have been buried yesterday, pale but waxy clean. The second was in a more advanced state of decay, blisters on its flesh where the fluids were trying to make their way to the surface. It's fat stomach a testament to roadkill bloat with a fly buzzing around its face.

A woman's voice called out to them. "If you're coming, come. Let's get this over with."

Olivia.

They walked forward, Dom with the knife high. Cans ready; Stephanie's thumb against the spark wheel. The corpse guards remained at their post, unmoving, staring straight ahead into nothing. Dom went for the fresher one, driving the combat knife deep into its stomach, while Stephanie used the hairspray like a flamethrower. Tom stepped in with the holy water when the two had collapsed onto the floor.

"Now why'd you do that?" Olivia asked. "They wouldn't have hurt a fly." She was sitting on the edge of her desk. Calm. As if she was waiting to discuss the next renovation in the building.

They stepped inside.

Tom moved forward, with Stephanie close behind, as Reilly entered last and closed the door behind them. Dom noted the man was living. Not a creature. Not one of the reanimated. He would take care of him later.

Olivia locked eyes with Dom. He sauntered to a side table, sheathed his knife and set down his pack.

She greeted him first. "I didn't know murderers could get parole."

"Attempted. You're still here, remember? For a little while."

She shifted her gaze. "Dear brother, how are you?" Her voice dripped with false sentiment. A slick honey gathered from toxic nectar. "How I've missed you."

"I'm here to give you a chance, Olivia."

She scoffed. "To do what?"

"Sever your ties with this demon. Walk away from evil."

"And, if I don't?" She slid to her feet, crossing her arms.

"Then I mean to perform an exorcism."

Laughter exploded around them. Her own and another, deeper sound that was felt more than heard. A dark vibration within their bones. The temperature in the room plummeted.

"How can you exorcise me when I'm not possessed? Are you mistaking the gifts he's given me as possession?"

Olivia reached into Tom's mind, knowing the buttons to push, the fears to twist. The memories to bring to the surface.

He was five again, standing at a child-sized easel in his mother's art room. She'd given him a small palette of colors and a paintbrush. He beamed at her, and she smiled.

"I love it when you paint with me, Tommy."

"Me, too, Mommy."

He returned to his canvas. He'd drawn his mother and tried to make their cat beside her, a whirlwind of brushstrokes, a black blur. Exactly how Jetty would appear before he became a cat.

The scene shifted as Olivia pulled it apart, manipulating time and space within his mind.

Jetty was there, growing into Black and becoming the thing that took his hand and destroyed his mother. They stood together as she backed away, begging, pleading for him to go to her.

But he didn't.

Olivia dug into the recesses of his mind and brought forth the moment he realized his Jetty had left him. His mother was gone. The crushing ache of being entirely alone and small in a world he didn't understand.

Tom winced. An emptiness filled him, eyes welling with tears. "Stop!" he hissed. "What you don't understand, *dear sister*, is this was what pulled me to the ministry. To my religion and my belief in God.

This set me on the path to where I am right now. Right here." He fought past the hollow ache in his chest. "This made me what I am."

"An insecure little man. Wrapping himself in shepherd's clothes out of fear, not belief."

"You're wrong," Stephanie said, coming to his aid.

"Oh? And you." She uncrossed her arms and pointed at the girl. "You trespassing little fool. Going where you don't belong, playing your game of chat with the dead." She focused on Stephanie, bringing up her memory of Seth's scream as he was sucked into the portal. Ripped through to the next realm. She played it over and over, scream after scream, until Stephanie pressed her hands against her ears.

She dropped to one knee. Terrified.

Dom reached into his pack, took out the board he'd made and put it on the table.

"And you," Olivia said, switching her focus.

"Don't try it, bitch. I've worked long and hard to keep you out of my head."

She tried. Probed. Sent thoughts, pulled memories. Of Amanda and the times they'd had investigating. Of his being responsible for her death. Brian's. Of his breakdown and spending weeks in a mental hospital, still never quite reconciling his guilt. His part in it all.

But he blocked her. Held his own.

She didn't know how he learned to keep her out. A shield, a wall. There were chinks in it. Small holes that she could weasel through, but she was tired of parlor tricks.

"You need to leave," she said. "Get out of my house." She dismissed them, shooing them out. "You've made enough of a mess here. It'll take days to clean up." She eyed them. "Go. While you still can." She waved her arm.

Stephanie looked up, recovering from the memory of Seth being ripped apart, the sound of his screams, and caught sight of the crow tattoo on Olivia's wrist. It had to be a connection to the things they'd fought. Would still be fighting if they wanted to get out of this place alive. She stood, inching closer to Tom.

Tom put his arm around Stephanie to make sure she was all right, and she whispered, "Look," as she tapped her wrist.

He saw. He acknowledged it with an almost imperceptible nod, then signaled Dom.

They ran at her. Stephanie caught Olivia around the waist, knocking her to the ground, while Tom seized her wrist, pinning it to the floor. Stephanie straddled Olivia, sitting on her and holding her other arm.

"Brutus!"

Reilly had his back against the door, watching everything unfold. She couldn't see him from where she was, but his choice had been made. He'd deal with the repercussions.

Olivia writhed and fought as Dom shoved between Stephanie and Tom, yanking his knife out of its sheath and stabbing it into the tattoo. It scraped bone as he pulled it out for another strike. Olivia screamed.

All the Morts in the building collapsed.

A shriek of pain and anger escaped her as her face shifted. Before Dom could swing the knife for a killing blow, it flew from his grasp and impaled itself into the floor. A force exploded outward from her, blasting all three in opposite directions.

Dom slammed into the wall, slumping to the floor and barely missing the knife. He caught his breath on all fours and used the table to pull himself upright. Tom hit the desk as Stephanie was thrown into a bookshelf.

"You bastard!" Olivia shrieked, grasping her wrist. Blood seeped between her fingers, dripping onto the floor. "Et tu, Brute, you lousy piece of shit. You're fucking fired." With a toss of her head, flames burned through his mind.

Reilly dropped to his knees. He could hear the crackling inside his skull. Smell flesh burning. Feel the charring of his mind. He held his head, his eyes squeezed shut. The pain, excruciating.

Dom slid the planchette from his pack.

"And you damn well need to put that thing away," she barked. Her wrist was a sticky, throbbing mess, the pain crawling up her arm, her hand tightened into a claw.

A dark shadow formed as the temperature plummeted. Condensation formed. Every exhale became a small cloud.

Tom turned to see what Olivia was talking about. "What the hell are you doing? A Ouija board? Here? Are you trying to undermine everything we're here to do?"

"What you're doing. I came with another purpose. I'm sending this demon to hell once and for all." He set the planchette on the board, resting his fingertips along its edge. The energy in the wood was an electricity that flowed through his hands, up into his arms and chest. "Now, my friend," he said. It's time."

The planchette slid to *Hello.*

Chapter 43

The area around Dom shook as a portal opened within his board. Tom grabbed Stephanie's arm and yanked her to the back of the room, away from Dom. From Olivia. From the mass forming above the board. He held her hands in his and began to pray.

Dom pressed his fingers onto the planchette as the current intensified, a tornado of force growing, along with a maniacal smile on his face. A being coalesced beside him, its icy hand on his shoulder. Talons rested along his collar bone. Amber eyes shined above its maw, a cavernous opening with razor sharp teeth. Acidic drool dripped to the floor, sizzling as it hit.

Tom's attention was drawn to the other side of the room while he recited Psalm 91. He backed Stephanie against the wall. "I will say of the Lord, 'He is my refuge and . . .'" His words were drowned out by a growl and a gathering of thousands of flies as the larger shadow loomed next to Olivia.

"This is what will take you out, you evil bastard!" Dom cried above the rumbling of the storm around them.

"Dom, your soul!" Tom shouted. "You'll be attached to this thing! Forever doomed! Send it back!"

"What's one compared to the countless souls who will be saved? I made my contract with this thing, and it's here to fulfill it's part of the bargain!"

The fire red eyes of the larger demon bore into Dom.

You are mistaken
Did you not realize

I command this realm

Black fixed his gaze onto the lesser demon.

Now

Dom's eyes went wild as its talons sank deep into his muscles and tendons severing them and breaking his collar bone. His scream echoed through the room. The ghoul twisted, sinking its teeth deep into Dom's neck and tearing it to shreds. Blood sprayed the walls as his being, soul, life force was pulled into the swirling mass and through the portal he'd created. His body collapsed, dragging the board to the floor.

Stephanie held onto Tom, gasping, nails digging into his arm. In his terror, he felt nothing.

Reilly tripped over a chair, mind still on fire, putting as much distance as he could between himself and what was happening. At the back of the room, his hand instinctively went to the gun he'd brought. The Glock was a protective weight in his hand, but he knew it wouldn't stop a savage specter.

Go

The lesser demon bowed and dissolved into the shadows.

Black turned toward Tom and Stephanie. Olivia followed suit.

Tom continued. His lips hadn't stopped, mind in an anxious loop of prayers. "You, unclean spirit, cannot harm myself, a minister, my assistant, our loved ones or any item belonging to us."

The shadow swayed as it watched him with unwavering burning eyes. Olivia was statue still beside it, arms at her sides. Her bleeding slowed, a pool of blood collected at her feet.

"If you stop this now, brother," she said, "we might let your girlfriend keep her soul. Not send her through the portal with the others."

"We will not stop. You are aligned with a thing of lies. Deceit. Evil. It cannot remain here."

"Do you really want to send her immortal soul to be torn to bits? Fed on? Like Seth's? Like your mother's?" She drew out the last word.

His mother's. He *had* seen her that night with the girls. She *had* reached out to him. And Olivia ended it. Taken her away. For the second time in his life, his mother had been stolen from him. He would not waiver now. Could not. This was for her.

"You will not distract me from my mission. I will pray for them. Each and every soul that your master has tried to destroy. But God will prevail." He touched his clerical collar, then pulled a cross from his pouch of vials. He held it high. "Saint Michael the Archangel, protect us . . ."

Brian listened to what was going on from the next room. He assumed Olivia had been too distracted to notice him. If he was ever going to take a stand, it had to be now. If they were going to have a chance to defeat this malignant fiend, he had to help. Now.

Olivia was done. She'd been patient with them, even when they killed her followers, but now her *brother* was trying to rid Black from his home. From her life. Strip her of her significance, her superiority. How dare he!

She bolted at him, hand outstretched to gouge out his eyes, whatever she had to do to stop him.

Reilly fired the gun, knocking her backward. Blood ran from the shoulder wound as she thrashed. She stumbled, trying to keep her balance. Another shot.

Brian barreled through the wall and seized the board from under Dom. Using every bit of force he could muster, every ounce of strength in his spirit, he flipped it toward her as she fell.

A shadow arm reached from the portal and reaped her soul. Wrested it from her dying body.

Stephanie realized she was still holding a can of hairspray. Digging a lighter out of her pocket, she stepped in front of Tom and aimed for the board. She guided the flame to its center, barely noticing the dark shape near her. An explosion thundered as the wooden board cracked into six misshapen pieces.

Black circled the room, a raging chaos. Pictures were thrown off the walls, light fixtures crashed down. A bookshelf fractured.

Brian took refuge behind the minister as he ducked down.

A picture of Olivia flew past Stephanie's head, glass shattering.

Tom recited every prayer they'd printed out, every prayer he'd memorized since he was a child. " . . . he drove out the spirits with a single word."

You are not He
Insignificant man

Another crash. Tom retrieved two vials from his pouch, holding one out to Stephanie. "Douse that board and get me the pieces."

She hesitated, hearing him but not comprehending, her eyes full of confusion and panic.

"You can do it, Steph. Plan B."

Those words snapped her back to the unreal reality that lay before her. She crawled to where the pieces of the board had landed.

Olivia's chair was thrown against the wall.

Tom sprayed the area around him with the holy water and the man stepped into the circle with him. Tom turned. "I assume you're with us?"

"I am." Reilly's mind had cooled. Cleared.

"Here." He shoved a vial into the man's hand. "Sparingly. We don't have a lot left."

Black waved a hand and sent a shard of glass at Tom, grazing his neck. Blood welled and dripped along his collar.

Remember killing Amanda
How it felt
To plunge that glass
Into her throat

The memories were a deluge, and Tom was submerged in them. Five. He was five years old, standing over his neighbor. Her ankle broken, cracked, from falling down the stairs. Her stomach was a mass of blood. The shears. She'd fallen on the shears. And none of that had mattered to him. All he wanted was his letter board.

She begged him, anguish and pain filling her voice. "Tommy, no."

And he'd taken that shard of glass, driving it into her throat. Taking her life. He'd killed her. He'd murdered his friend.

At five years old.

The memory crushed him. Drove him to his knees. That he killed her. That he had it in his being to murder someone.

And yet he had. That something within him had been Jet. Jetty. *Black.*

It hadn't been his fault. It hadn't even been him. It was the cancerous pus-filled evil that stood before him.

He pulled himself to his feet, dragged himself out of the despair that the demon had thought would take him down.

"Not today, Satan.

Black whipped around, sending Olivia's desk at him. Reilly and Tom jumped out of the way.

"You cannot harm myself or assistants, and you will submit to my authority!"

A gravelly laugh, louder than before, shook the walls and a vile sewer-stench filled the room.

You have no authority
Leave me

He threw Tom against the wall and vanished.

Chapter 44

Stephanie ran to Tom, dropping the pieces of the Ouija board on the floor beside him. Reilly stood over them.

"Are you okay?" She brushed hair away from his face, checking his chest, arms, legs. Making sure he wasn't hurt. Making sure he was alive.

Blood dripped from a cut on the back of his head, and the wind was knocked out of his lungs. "I'm all right. I'm all right." He sat up, a hand on his chest. He coughed. "That was a doozy." Pain coursed through his skull.

"It's gone. We can leave." Reilly put away his gun.

Tom shook his head. "It's not. This is the eye of the storm. If we leave now, he wins. Continues. We've got to finish this." Stephanie took his arm, helping him to stand.

Brian felt helpless in his spectral form. He hovered close, keeping a watch for the demon. It was the only thing he could do.

Reilly spoke again. "We need to go, and this place needs to be demolished."

"Do you really think that demon would leave, even if the building was gone?" He was incredulous. "That monster will never leave unless we do something about it."

"And what do you suggest? Your exorcism fell kind of short."

Stephanie scowled at him. "Don't be an asshole. You're still alive, aren't you?"

"And how is that his doing?"

Tom let go of Stephanie, his back straight. "Go if you want. We've got this."

Reilly averted his eyes, wanting to run. Unsure of what to do. He'd sunk himself into this hole. Didn't know if he could dig himself out. Didn't know if that thing would ever let him go.

"Do we?" she asked Tom. "Do we have this?"

He took her hand and squeezed. "We've got Plan B."

"Give me the pieces of the board."

Stephanie gathered up the fragments, counting them. "Six. Here you go." She handed them over. Tom arranged them on the table in front of him. Reilly moved in close, surveying the situation.

"What's Plan B?"

"I need to concentrate. Can you two wait in the hall while I get this ready?"

Stephanie nodded and motioned to Reilly to join her. He went, glancing over his shoulder to catch a glimpse of what Tom was doing. The door swung shut behind them.

Tom held his hands over the pieces, sensing their leftover energy. The negativity with which the wood had been infused. Remnants of the portal. He needed to cleanse and reverse it. Clear its energy if this was going to work.

"Plan B." He'd give it the old college try. Unzipping the bottom compartment of his bag, a few little things tumbled onto the table: small wad of sage, some crystals. A Ziplock bag of blessed salt. A few things he picked up from Everything Eclectic the last time he passed through Centerville. He flicked the lighter Stephanie left on the table and lit the sage.

None of this was in his wheelhouse. But neither was battling a demon on the site of an old asylum. He held each fragment in the smoke of the sage, turning and covering every inch. Setting the pieces in a circle on the table, he used the salt to cover them. He hoped it was enough.

Crystals at the corners, surrounding the broken board. Hands above.

He hoped God was still on his side and his internet research was correct.

Tom began to chant.

Slowly, the pieces twisted, melding into one solid shape.

Reilly was growing antsy, an anxiety rising in his chest with every breath. He paced the short distance from Stephanie to the light fixture, back. Again. Again. "How long is he gonna be?"

She shrugged. "As long as it takes."

"What's he doing?"

"I don't know."

"Look," he said on his next pass beside her, "we need to get out of here. Before that thing returns. We can walk out, into the sunlight and away from this place. Leave it in the dust."

He took her by the arm, and she yanked it away from him.

"I'm staying."

"He doesn't need us. He's got his own Plan B."

"I'm not going."

He held up his palms. "Suit yourself."

With that, the door to the office opened and Tom stepped out. In his hand was a small wooden box. One side was open, and he carried the matching piece in his other hand.

"A box?" Reilly scoffed. He was so far past finished with this. It was ridiculous. They were idiots for wasting their time "A box. That's your big plan? I'm outta here."

"No one's stopping you. Just tell me," he said, "where has this abomination set up shop? Is there a room, an area, anywhere that's its own?"

Reilly walked backwards, away from them. "It's behind you,

man. That door at the end of the hall. Has an altar and everything. Olivia called it the Sanctuary."

Tom looked at Stephanie. "That's exactly what I need."

"I am out." He pointed finger guns at the two. "Good luck. Have fun."

"Have a nice life." Stephanie couldn't contain her annoyance.

Reilly gave her the finger as they moved toward the demon's hideaway. Its dwelling. Lair. Nothing made it sound or feel any better. He hoped to be far away before the thing noticed he was gone.

Tom arrived at the door and, with no hesitation, threw it open.

A wind tore past them with a howl as a dark tentacle pinpointed Reilly, encircled him and tightened like a boa constrictor. It twisted around his neck and his chest, squeezing until all the blood vessels in his body burst and his lungs flamed. Yellow and white lights like fireworks exploded in his eyes before it all went black.

Tom and Stephanie stepped into Black's sanctum.

Tom spun on his heel, box in hand, arm outstretched, as the demon filled the room. Stephanie tried to get behind Tom as something wrapped around her and threw her to the other side of the room. She crumbled to the floor.

Black's Ouija board lay on an altar draped in red. The demon stood before it. A planchette materialized above the board then dropped, going to letters that Tom couldn't read. Ancient ruins instead of an alphabet. Black raised his arms as a portal opened. An odor of death emanated from the vortex, and Tom could see shadow arms grappling, trying to climb out and into this realm.

He chanted. The words he said giving the box its power. He inched closer to Black as the energy in the room crackled and spun around them. An evil wind, dark and chattering, fought his foothold. It pulled at his being as the box sought the malignant spirit in front of him.

Today you die
Tommy

The familiar voice said his name, trying to make him falter. Draw him back to his childhood pain. But he was steadfast. Let it play its tricks. His arm remained outstretched. The energy of the portal filled the room, swirling and fetid. Dark creatures crawled from the portal and scuttled at his feet, scratching and clawing. Biting. His ankles burned as the evil ripped his flesh, his sneakers damp with blood. Sticky with their saliva.

Another inch. Black's fire red eyes bored into his own, into his mind, sending tendrils of poison into his thoughts while disintegrating his retinas.

Step closer to the board
Tommy
Your fate was sealed long ago

"The Lord is my refuge and my fortress!"

He lost his footing, tripping on one of the ghouls, and slammed into the altar. With all his might, he held onto the edge of the table. Demons pulled at his legs, trying to drag him into the portal to a realm of damnation. Of forever terror. It was sucking his strength, devouring his breath. His lifeforce. He was losing. In moments he'd be torn apart, and Black would celebrate. Claim victory.

Despair crept into his soul.

Brian materialized at the altar. In one motion, he sent the board flying and grabbed the box from Tom, jamming it into Black's ribcage like a knife.

Tom collapsed as the demon thundered.

His minions brayed.

The portal closed.

Black writhed and twisted, an ungodly growl emanating from deep within his being, as he was dragged into the box. Brian crouched beside Tom, taking the final side of the cube from the floor at his feet. He held it in place where it settled seamlessly, imprisoning the demon.

Brian tucked the cube into Tom's hands and faded, spent.

Stephanie came to. Her head was throbbing, and her body ached. She saw Tom keeled over in front of the altar. He'd aged. His hair was a pale shade of grey and his eyes were sunken. His skin seemed translucent and so thin she could see his blue veins. She crawled to him, lifting his head onto her lap. His breathing was shallow. She prayed everything was over.

As she held him, a man's voice came from the hallway.

"Oh, my God."

She could barely muster, "Help us," and burst into tears as Bob Walters entered the room, gun drawn. "Please, help us."

Walters took out his cellphone and dialed 911. He wrapped Stephanie in his jacket and pulled the drape off the altar for Tom. Tom. The man in front of him could've been Tom's grandfather, drawn and frail.

He'd already seen his friend. Kneeled beside Dom, who'd been ripped apart by only God knew what. He knew, though. God help him, he knew.

"How did you know where we were?" Stephanie asked. She was shaking, shivering.

"I called Tom, but he didn't answer. So, I checked his location. He never turned it off from when we met at the hotel." His voice cracked.

Walters stood at the doorway as they waited for the ambulance.

Epilogue

Four Weeks Later

The nurses' station hummed, and machines beeped. Equipment lined the hallway of Hilldale Hospital's seventh floor oncology ward. Janice Ortega walked into the room of the new patient on the floor, Reverend Thomas Anderson. He'd been moved from the general wing to begin an aggressive chemotherapy regimen.

"Good morning, Pastor. My name is Janice, and I'll be taking care of you." She checked his IV bags and lines, then his bracelet. "That's odd." She looked into his face. "The birth date on your bracelet says you're twenty-eight. Now we both know that's not right, don't we?" She couldn't believe he'd been shuffled around the hospital with the wrong date on his wrist. It had to be a typo on the year. She knew he wasn't a day younger than eighty-five. Eighty-seven, even. "No worries, hon. I'll get that fixed and then I'll start your chemo when we're sure everything's right."

Tom said nothing. Saw nothing. He was in a world of darkness, and everything was numb. No thought. No life. A sickness brewed in him since Black touched his mind, but he was a lifeless shell, confined in the way he had bound the demon into his box. The boundaries were the same. The tradeoff immutable. He hadn't been sure of the words he'd chanted, only that they would make a cell. A prison. A room with no view. He hadn't realized he'd be locked away as well. Somewhere.

The nurse moved his bedside tray out of her way, knocking a small wooden box to the floor. "Oops. Sorry." She returned it to the tray. "Not sure what it is, but they told me you came in clutching it. It's safe right here." She patted the tray. "Don't you worry. I'll be back when I get your birth date fixed. I don't know how they let this slip."

She left, stopping at the nurses' station to complain about the error.

Black flexed, the walls of his confinement pressing back at him. He'd never experienced anything like this before and was curious. Another stretch, pushing the limits of his locality. The walls expanded, a little, then settled. Patience was key.

He breathed. There were a few souls he hadn't yet feasted on from the essences that Olivia had brought him. Seth. The woman called Lilith. He tightened into a ball and sent out his reach, drawing them into him. Taking their fear and dread into his being, swallowing it whole. It energized him. His reward for putting up with that girl for so long.

A larger flex, a concentrated *push* outward.

He heard crumbling, like pebbles on concrete. The breaking down of the man's feeble attempt to hold him. A hairline crack appeared on the wall. Fissures, spidering out from the center, letting a faint light through.

His maw widened into a death grin.

The man's insecurities, inexperience, *inadequacy* had left their marks on his prison. Made the binding useless.

A last stretch and the edges of the cracks chipped away. He waited as the walls disintegrated. The binding exploded, and Black sent fragments of the box outward into the world, as each one reconstructed. Each becoming a separate Ouija board.

The demon expanded to its full self, seven feet of buzzing fly darkness, and glared at the broken man in the bed.

Tommy

The overwhelming fear that slammed into Tom's brain made his body stir, his legs twist in the hospital sheets. Adrenalin filled a body that couldn't move.

And then Black screamed into his mind. He raised his arm and the switches to Tom's IV turned, pouring chemicals into his veins. The machines monitoring the man sounded their alarms as seizures racked his body and his heart stopped.

Black cloaked himself in darkness and left to roam the night.

ABOUT THE AUTHOR

Barb Shadow is a paranormal investigator and researcher, living with her family on the East Coast. She founded the Sullivan Paranormal Society, an investigative team in upstate New York, and has appeared on numerous radio shows to discuss her experiences. When not writing spine-tingling tales, you can find Barb with headphones on, listening for EVPs from her team's latest investigations.

If you've had a paranormal experience and would like to share it with Barb or have it considered for inclusion in an upcoming anthology, you can submit it on the From the Shadows Publishing website, **fromtheshadowspublishing.com**.

www.ingramcontent.com/pod-product-compliance
Lightning Source LLC
Chambersburg PA
CBHW052041240626
47153CB00006B/2181